"Kirk,

"What do you mean, stop? Honey, what's the matter with you? All of a sudden you're stiff as a board."

Holly was fighting to catch her breath. "I can't—I can't do this, Kirk. No platform romances. Not with you or anyone else."

He sat up then, flushed. "You're serious, aren't you?"

"You're not the first man on board a rig to make a pass, and I don't suppose you'll be the last. I'm not going to let any of you ruin my career." But how could she forget the flame he'd ignited, the embers of desire that would not die away . . . ?

ERIN ROSS

has pursued a wide variety of activities during her life. At one time or another, this author studied radio, taught guitar, practiced karate and sang with a rock group. But writing has always been a favorite pursuit. "I'm an avid reader," she explains, "and I think sooner or later all avid readers get the bug to write!"

Dear Reader:

SILHOUETTE DESIRE is an exciting new line of contemporary romances from Silhouette Books. During the past year, many Silhouette readers have written in telling us what other types of stories they'd like to read from Silhouette, and we've kept these comments and suggestions in mind in developing SILHOUETTE DESIRE.

DESIREs feature all of the elements you like to see in a romance, plus a more sensual, provocative story. So if you want to experience all the excitement, passion and joy of falling in love, then SILHOUETTE DESIRE is for you.

Karen Solem
Editor-in-Chief
Silhouette Books

ERIN ROSS
ROSS
Tide's End

Silhouette Desire
Published by Silhouette Books New York
America's Publisher of Contemporary Romance

Silhouette Books by Erin Ross

Second Harvest (DES #18)
Flower of the Orient (SE #107)
Time for Tomorrow (DES #89)
Fragrant Harbor (DES #114)
Tide's End (DES #137)

SILHOUETTE BOOKS, a Division of Simon & Schuster, Inc.
1230 Avenue of the Americas, New York, N.Y. 10020

Copyright © 1984 by Erin Ross

Distributed by Pocket Books

ISBN: 0-671-49574-7

First Silhouette Books printing May, 1984

10 9 8 7 6 5 4 3 2 1

SILHOUETTE, SILHOUETTE DESIRE and colophon are
registered trademarks of Simon & Schuster, Inc.

America's Publisher of Contemporary Romance

Printed in the U.S.A.

BC91

To my daughter, Holly.
With very special thanks to: Linda (L.L.) Palmer,
Senior Chemical Engineer, Chevron U.S.A., Inc.;
John F. Manuel, Manager, Ocean Systems,
Lockheed Missiles & Space Company, Inc., and
"The Prince."

Tide's End

1

Holly Bishop was cold. She was also tired, hungry and angry with herself. All of which, she admitted ruefully, did not make for a particularly inspiring morning.

She stood back as the crew began the tedious operation of tripping out, or changing the drill bit at the end of the mile-long pipe. Mentally she kicked herself for giving in to temptation the night before. She'd known about this morning's 5 A.M. call, yet she'd gone ahead and watched that old James Bond movie anyway. Sin in haste, repent at leisure. Even 007 wasn't worth the ragged way she felt this morning after less than four hours sleep!

Holly ducked as a clump of mud got loose from one of the pipes and came flying in her direction. "Watch out, Holly girl," she mumbled under her breath. "The old reflexes aren't what they should be this morning."

But then without her morning coffee what could she

9

expect? She'd awakened only twenty minutes ago, too late to do anything but brush her teeth, throw on her clothes and rush on deck for the beginning of her twelve-hour shift. Holly shivered at a sudden gust of wind. Now it looked as if it was going to be a long morning, she thought, pulling her jacket more tightly around her shoulders—a *very* long morning!

As the men continued to pull length after length of pipe from the steel and concrete casing, she leaned back against a guardrail and reflected on her present situation. What was she, Holly Marie Bishop, twenty-seven years old, reasonably attractive, practical minded—last night's madness excluded—doing standing on top of an eighteen-story oil rig positioned more then twenty miles off the coast of Morro Bay, California? Her eyes burned from lack of sleep, her nose felt like a popsicle, her head throbbed from the deafening roar of the machinery. Yet here she stood, the only female aboard an otherwise all-male rig, ching as a crew of drillers, roughnecks and roustabouts changed a dull bit at the end of more than a mile of pipe. Incredible!

"You look as if you could use a cup of coffee," a familiar voice drawled. "What's the matter? Wind keep you awake last night?"

Holly turned to find Carl Morris grinning down at her, soft brown eyes twinkling in a deeply tanned, pleasantly rugged face. Five-foot-ten, balding, portly but not exactly fat, Carl was toolpusher on Platform Kathy. As usual, he wore a bright plaid shirt, faded jeans and an ancient, scuffed pair of cowboy boots.

At fifty-five, Carl had spent nearly thirty years aboard offshore oil rigs from the North Sea to the coast of California. His official job as toolpusher required him to supervise the drilling crew. Unofficially, he was friend-to-all, father confessor and, in the case of any females working aboard the rig, self-appointed protector, a role which had earned him the affectionate title, "Prince of Passion." Since she'd come on board six months ago, Carl had taken Holly under his wing like an overzealous brood hen.

"It wasn't the wind," she answered, looking up at him sheepishly. "It was Sean Connery. This morning I have lived to regret my indiscretion."

"You may regret it even more by the time the copter gets here." She really did look tired, he thought. Not a very promising way to meet the boss. "Tell you what. When we get through tripping out I'll buy you a cup of coffee."

"By the time you make your way through all that pipe it'll be too late. As soon as I check on the mud I'm going to grab a quick cup before I become the only employee in Worldwide's history to walk overboard in her sleep."

"Come on, mud mama," he teased. "Are you telling me a woman can't take these hours as well as a man?"

"No way," she told him, not at all put off by the unflattering sobriquet. "I'm just saying that this woman is too darn susceptible to Sean Connery's charms."

As chemical engineer and drilling representative for Worldwide Oil, one of Holly's responsibilities was to monitor the specially formulated mud mixture that was forced through the drill stem to cool and lubricate the bit. Since Kathy's completion a year ago, four wells had been drilled off the platform. Because it was to be a forty-eight-slot rig, the drilling would continue for at least two more years. During that time, Holly would spend part of each day testing and analysing the chemical and physical properties of the drilling fluid. Men who performed this duty were called "mud engineers." Inevitably a woman with the same job became a "mud mama."

"Speaking of charms," Carl went on, "looks like you've put a good one on the boss. I don't like the way Hohlman eyed you the last time he was on board."

Despite the brisk morning, Holly felt a sudden flash of heat. Carl wasn't the only one who'd been put off by Sid Hohlman's leers. The man was becoming a downright pain in the neck. Ever since her name had been proposed as drilling rep for the Morro Bay project, the regional manager had lost no opportunity to let her know how instrumental he could be in getting her the job. When she refused all offers to see him after work hours, he'd become so unpleasant that she'd finally put tact aside and told him the truth. If dating him was a prerequisite for getting the job, he knew what he could do with it!

One week later she'd been assigned to Platform Kathy, proof that her ability alone was enough to win her the job. Unfortunately, an even larger dose of Sid Hohlman seemed to come with the promotion. The regional manager used the flimsiest excuses to visit the rig, and once there, blithely continued his campaign of sexual harassment. It was tiring and it was insulting. Still, because she was so new on her job, Holly hesitated to lodge a formal complaint. So far her only defense had been to stay as far away from him as possible—a tactic that was proving increasingly difficult to implement.

"I figure to keep an eye on him this morning, so he'd better watch his step," Carl went on.

Holly gave a little groan. "I should have known he'd

be on board. Why's he coming this time, Carl? He was just here the day before yesterday. Doesn't he think this rig can run without him?"

Carl gave a snort. "He doesn't think the *world* can run without him. Everytime he comes out here it takes a whole shift to recover from the visit. But this time he's got visitors, and heaven forbid any VIP should come on board without Hohlman hovering over him like a guardian angel."

"Visitors?" Holly's heart sank further. As resident expert it was her job to guide visitors around the rig. It was the last thing she felt like doing this morning. "Do you know who they are?"

Carl nodded his head and reached into his shirt pocket for the ever-present packet of chewing tobacco he kept stored there. Holly winced as he tore off a healthy-size chew, knowing that the mixture had been liberally sprinkled with hot sauce. At this hour of the morning she wondered how his stomach could stand it.

Carl pushed the chew to one side of his mouth and said, "One of them is that reporter fellow from the *Morro Bay Weekly.* I think the head of the local fishermen's association's coming too. Oh, and Kirk Roberts will be on board. I hear they've contracted his diving company to do the quarterly platform inspection."

If it was possible for Holly's spirits to plummet any further, they did at the mention of the first two visitors. Kirk Roberts she knew by reputation only. Because Roberts's crew had been working in the hazardous waters off Aberdeen, Scotland, for the past few years, she'd never actually met the diver.

Secretly she wished she could say the same for the other visitors. Mike Rafferty was one of the *Morro Bay*

Weekly's top reporters and was notoriously unsympathetic to offshore drilling. Mario Palermo represented the local fishermen. Since Holly frequently worked with Mario's daughter, Ginny, during her off-duty hours on shore, she knew of his concern that the drilling might hurt the coastal fishing industry. Both men would have to be handled patiently and with tact, a job she wasn't sure she was up to at six in the morning. Darn you, Sean Connery, she thought irritably. Now look where you've landed me!

It wasn't difficult to read Holly's thoughts, and Carl chuckled. "Come on, don't look so glum. You always do a great job of handling these guys." He aimed a wad of tobacco at an empty can some ten feet away, hitting it with perfect accuracy. "And if that guy Hohlman bothers you again just say the word and I'll arrange a little unexpected swim for him. That ought to cool him off."

Holly couldn't help smiling. "Carl, you're a sweetheart." She reached up and kissed him on the cheek. "I don't know what I'd do without you."

Carl's suntanned face grew even redder. "That's what I've been trying to tell you for the past six months," he told her with a self-conscious grin. The wad of tobacco shifted to the other cheek. "Guess I'd better get back to work before those guys twist that pipe into a pretzel. Are you going to take a sample now?"

"I might as well. Then I can go to the crew's quarters and change my clothes." She looked down at her functional, unflattering work clothes. Like Carl, her feet were encased in steel-toed cowboy boots, her head in a regulation hard hat. She also wore a pair of faded jeans, sweat shirt and a blue nylon-cord man's jacket. Beneath the hard hat she'd tied a bright yellow bandana in a largely unsuccessful attempt to contain her unruly dark brown hair. Not glamorous. No, definitely not the kind of outfit one wore to greet the press. "By the way, when do you expect our esteemed visitors to arrive?"

Carl shrugged. "Your guess is as good as mine. If I know Hohlman—and I try very hard *not* to—he'll arrive just in time to catch us off guard." He winked. "Some people never learn. If *we* look bad, *he* looks bad."

Holly rolled her eyes in agreement and followed Carl over to the rotary drill system, but was distracted by a loud racket overhead. Looking up, she saw "Lucy," the company Agusta 109 helicopter hovering in a whirl of wind just above the helideck. As it came slowly down, she spotted the familiar figure of the company pilot along with several other passengers in the six-man cockpit. With a little groan, she saw that one of them was the regional manager, Sid Hohlman. Damn, they were here. And she hadn't even had time to change her clothes!

With a resigned shrug, she mouthed the words, "Here we go again," at Carl, then moved around the drilling apparatus to wait for the visitors to step down to the main deck of the platform.

Sid Hohlman was the first man off the helicopter. Of medium height, overweight, with straight, mousy-brown hair, the regional manager was, as usual, wearing a perfectly tailored three-piece suit. Holly could only suppose that the outfit was worn to impress the crew. In reality it had become a company joke. To come aboard an oil platform dressed for a company board meeting was the height of idiocy. Holly's mouth twitched. But maybe that was explanation enough, she thought unkindly.

Next to deplane was Mike Rafferty of the *Morro Bay Weekly*. Pencil thin, with longish brown hair and beard, the reporter was dressed practically in jeans and a sweat shirt. Over his shoulder was slung the ever-present press camera. Behind him came Mario Palermo, the short, nervous, roly-poly head of the Morro Bay Fishermen's Association.

Holly was about to turn away when the fourth man stepped out of the helicopter. Maybe it was the early morning hour, or perhaps it was her lack of sleep the night before, but Holly thought she'd never seen a more handsome male. As he awaited his turn to descend the metal stairs leading down to the main deck, he stood spotlighted by the sun, and for an electric moment Holly had the feeling she was looking up at some sort of golden god.

She blinked and looked again. He was still there, poised above her larger than life. Then the god smiled and Holly felt as if the sun had deserted the heavens to take on human form. And to think that bygone maidens had sacrificed themselves to lesser idols!

The most striking thing about him was his hair, she decided. It really was remarkable; thick, windblown and very blond, it formed a shiny golden halo as it flew about his tanned face.

And that face! Not precisely model-perfect, it had a quality that would make any woman look twice. Yet as he descended the stairs she could find no single feature which was truly spectacular. Unless it was his eyes. An unusual shade of aquamarine, they seemed to reflect the early morning sea. More important, she detected a strong glint of humor, as if he didn't take himself or his companions too seriously. She liked that.

His face was square-shaped and very tan. His

shoulders were unusually broad and she could see the power in his arms despite the long-sleeve shirt he was wearing. His nose was straight, his cheekbones high and well defined, his jaw set in a firm, almost stubborn line. Holly decided she liked that, too. All in all, he was not the sort of man who stepped off Lucy every day. If this was Kirk Roberts, the diver Carl was expecting, then maybe the day wasn't going to be so bad after all!

"Honey, you know Mike Rafferty and Mario Palermo, don't you?"

Holly started as Sid Hohlman slipped a proprietary arm around her waist. He nodded at the fourth man. "And this is Kirk Roberts. His company will be doing our platform inspections. Kirk, this is Holly Bishop, the cutest little mud mama west of the Mississippi."

Holly smiled despite gritted teeth and tried to squirm gracefully out of Sid Hohlman's embrace. His grip tightened imperceptibly; he was not going to let her go. The man's nerve was beyond belief! He'd known she wouldn't create a scene in front of visitors, and he'd unashamedly used that knowledge to his advantage.

Admitting temporary defeat, Holly flashed Hohlman a baleful look and reached out her hand to the others. "It's good to see you again, Mike, Mr. Palermo. And I'm glad to meet you, Mr. Roberts. I've heard a lot about your company."

Kirk Roberts felt a tingle like an electric shock when he touched Holly Bishop's hand. He looked with interest at the small oval face beneath the hard hat and was surprised. Her skin was clear and smooth and evenly tanned, her large, blue-gray eyes perfectly spaced between gracefully arched brows. He could see by the tendrils which had come loose from beneath her scarf that her hair was dark brown, and as he watched it blow about her face he detected rich, deep auburn highlights. Despite the ill-fitting men's work clothes, the woman was beautiful. Not at all what he had expected to find at the end of his six thousand-mile journey.

"The pleasure's mine, Miss Bishop," he said, and meant it. Then he looked at Sid Hohlman's hand held tightly on her waist and wondered at their relationship. It would be a shame if she was already taken.

Holly was delighted to discover that Kirk Roberts's voice was as attractive as the rest of him. It was low and well-modulated, but there was a spontaneous quality there too, as if he really were glad to meet her. Then she saw his eyes drop curiously to the manager's intimate grip on her waist and she flushed. Perhaps if her boss hadn't chosen that exact moment to give her an extra little squeeze—showing off his possession no doubt—she probably could have held her temper in check. But when Holly saw that knowing smile curve Kirk Roberts's mouth, she felt a rush of justifiable rage. She knew what the diver was thinking, she could see it written on his face just as clearly as if it were emblazoned there in neon letters.

Even then she probably could have handled the situation more tactfully—although with hindsight she couldn't think how. There were just some people in this world who had to have a house drop on them to get the point. For once Holly simply did what came naturally. And what felt most natural—indeed felt absolutely *exquisite* at that moment—was to raise her right foot and aim one pointed, steel-toed boot at Sid Hohlman's shins.

Seldom had Holly been more gratified than with the howl this simple action elicited. Pulling his arm from her waist as if it had been burnt, Hohlman used both hands to massage his afflicted limb. Affecting a look of innocence, Holly looked down and said sweetly, "Oh, I'm so sorry, Mr. Hohlman. The deck was oily and my foot slipped. I hope I didn't hurt your leg?"

"It's all right," the manager said through clenched teeth, the pained look on his face announcing that it wasn't anything of the sort. His dark, protruding eyes flashed at her as if daring her to contradict him. "I'm sure it was an accident."

Holly supressed the urge to laugh. Now Hohlman was the one who couldn't afford to make a scene in front of visitors, especially a visiting reporter. Later, when they were alone—well, she'd have to face that moment when it came. For now she was content that at least one of the three visitors understood that it had been no accident.

And there was no doubt in her mind that he understood. Over Sid Hohlman's bobbing head, she caught sight of the smiling eyes, the amused grin that shared in her triumph. Kirk Roberts knew all right. Only why, she wondered abruptly, should she care one iota whether he did or not?

"I didn't know they taught maneuvers like that in engineering school."

Holly turned to find the diver walking behind her on the way to the "dog house," or platform office. For the past two hours she'd shown the visitors the ins and outs and ups and downs of Platform Kathy. Throughout the tour Mike Rafferty had snapped away with his camera—hardly a nut or bolt escaped his notice—while Mario Palermo seemed in mortal fear that the rig might suffer a major blowout at any moment. Sid Hohlman pouted, and Kirk Roberts—well, Kirk Roberts continued to be just plain distracting.

The reporter had been trying to talk her into posing for a picture next to Hook Harrigan's nude June calendar pinup when Holly had been called to the phone in the platform office. Thanking whatever fates had seen fit to save her, she had gratefully left the men to ogle Miss June without her restrictive presence, unaware that Kirk Roberts had left the crew quarters behind her. She wondered what he wanted.

"When you're one of the few women in your engineering classes you'd be surprised what you learn," Holly said smiling. She gave him a sidelong look as they walked. There was no doubt about it. The man was a decided improvement to the platform scenery.

"Does that mean you give all your admirers that kind of treatment?"

"In the first place," she said, continuing toward the dog house, "Sid Hohlman is not an admirer, he's a wolf in executive clothing. Secondly, that depends."

He grinned. "Okay, I'll bite. On what?"

Holly noted that he had a terrific smile. "On who's doing the admiring."

"Hmmm, I see."

He seemed to be digesting this as they made their way around a circle of friction blocks that were undergoing repair. When he failed to say anything else she stopped behind the Elliott raft, stored for emergencies in its large white barrel, and looked up at him. "Mr. Roberts, why are you following me?"

Roberts leaned against the barrel and looked down at her. He wondered if she was really so ignorant of her charms that she could ask that question. "Kirk. And would you believe it's because I like the way you look in jeans and a hard hat?"

Holly gave him a disparaging smile. "I think you can do better than that."

"I probably could if you'd give me a little time to work on it."

"Sorry. Time is the one thing I don't have right now." She nodded toward the office. "I've got a call, remember?"

"In a minute." He put a hand on her shoulder, and Holly was surprised to feel the most peculiar prickling sensations run down her arm. Very strange, she thought. She couldn't remember that happening before. "Why do you let him get away with it?" he asked unexpectedly.

"Him?" Those eyes were very disruptive to normal brain function, she decided.

"Hohlman."

"Oh." Holly had absolutely no desire to discuss her regional manager. In fact she made it a point to think of him as little as possible. "I'm afraid Sid Hohlman comes with the territory. You know, like the mud pit and dull bits. You learn to handle him after a while."

His grin spread. He liked the way her eyes nearly matched the blue sky behind her, and the way her nose twitched slightly when she was annoyed. "Like kicking him in the shins?"

Holly winced. "Okay, I'll admit that was a bit drastic. Normally, I can control the situation less dramatically." The same way you're handling *this* situation? a little voice asked. In case you hadn't noticed, his hand is still on your shoulder! Aloud she said, "Mr. Roberts, your hand is still on my shoulder."

"Kirk. And I know." He showed not the slightest interest in removing it. Instead, he brushed the fingers of his other hand down the side of her face, and the hot prickles from her arm spread to the new location

21

like wildfire. Unless she was mistaken, she was about to get her second pass of the day.

"Would it—would it be asking too much of you to remove your hand?" Was she imagining it or was his mouth closer now then it had been?

"Yes, it would," he said. There was no doubt about it, his mouth had definitely passed the safety point. And it was still moving in.

"I think it's only fair to warn you that I—" she cleared her throat—"that I can kick with my right boot or my left." Strange, she thought, there seemed to be something caught in her throat that was making it difficult to breathe.

"You've got very talented feet." His lips had moved well into the danger zone.

The madness of the situation hit her one-eighth of a second before his lips did. Above the pervading smell of oil and diesel fuel she caught the faint, delicious scent of lemon and fresh mint which still lingered on his skin. Unfair tactics, she thought vaguely. Anyone who can cause sensations like this should be declared a public hazard!

She raised one foot in self-defense, but it stubbornly refused to cooperate. Instead it hung suspended while his kiss grew more insistent. Of course it might not be a bad idea—out of scientific curiosity, she thought hazily —to explore the situation a little further. There was no doubt the feelings she was experiencing now were a world apart from the ones she'd felt earlier toward her boss.

Her skin felt startlingly alive where his breath fanned her face, and the not unpleasant stirring in the lower region of her body seemed to be getting more pronounced. She was intensely aware of the hard muscles which were pressing through the material of her jacket, and of the heat he was generating—and that she was assimilating. For a few moments Platform Kathy seemed not to exist. Even the harsh grind of machinery was forgotten as she melted into his arms.

Then she heard one of the roughnecks call out and the spell was broken. The sights, smells and sounds of the rig came crashing down upon her, a jolting reminder that only a narrow white barrel separated them from the full view of the drilling crew.

"Wait a minute," she cried, pulling out of his arms. "This has gone way too far." Holly stood for a moment trying to catch her breath. His hands were still circling her waist lightly, and he was looking down at her with a peculiar half smile on his handsome face. Even though she had broken off the kiss, her blood continued to pound hard in her veins. She swallowed with difficulty and realized that her mouth felt like a dry wad of cotton.

"This is an oil rig, remember, not the beach at Waikiki," she went on, trying to make light of what had passed between them. When he continued to smile silently down at her she nodded toward the office. "My call—whoever it is will think I've fallen overboard."

He seemed not to have heard. "You know something?" he said with that annoying, irrepressible grin of his. "Underneath that hard hat I suspect there lurks a very lovely and desirable woman."

Holly took a deep breath. "Underneath this hat lurks an engineer who'd better stop talking and get back to her work," she told him in her best I-am-in-charge-here voice. She started to pass him but he was blocking the narrow path to the dog house. Holly looked up at him pointedly.

He stepped back lazily, but not quite far enough to

allow her to pass unobstructed. "Be my guest," he told her amicably.

Holly hesitated a moment then walked around him, brushing her shoulder against his chest in the process. She didn't stop, but continued toward the dog house, aware that her heart was beating more rapidly then the slight touch warranted.

She heard a soft chuckle behind her back, and the sound, a low, seductive counterpoint to the whine of machinery, stayed with her all the way to the office.

"I assure you there is absolutely no danger of an oil spill. Worldwide Oil has taken every precaution to prevent even the remotest chance of an accident. Here, let me explain—"

Holly tuned out. Whenever Sid Hohlman was on his soap box she tuned out. And he had been perched there for nearly two hours now, which was, by Holly's reckoning, about one hundred and fifteen minutes longer than any human being should be asked to suffer.

For the umpteenth time she found herself looking around for Kirk Roberts. She hadn't seen him since she'd left him behind the Elliott raft. He'd been nowhere in sight when she'd finished with her call, and the tour had gone on without him.

Unfortunately, in Kirk Roberts's case at least, out of sight did not necessarily mean out of mind. Holly was finding it difficult to forget the way his eyes had raked over her with a kind of provocative insolence, or the way she'd felt in his arms. And those lips—

"Miss Bishop. Mr. Rafferty asked you a question."

Holly was jarred out of her thoughts to find Sid Hohlman glaring at her, while the reporter stood with his pencil poised above his note pad. "I'm sorry, Mike. I'm afraid I didn't catch what you said."

"We've heard Mr. Hohlman's views on the subject, now I'd like to know what you think about safety precautions aboard the platform. Are they as fool-proof as your manager here seems to think?"

Holly glanced quickly at her boss. She could see by the look on his face that he expected her to back him up a hundred percent. The fact of the matter was, of course, that no matter how many precautions one took, occasionally an accident did happen. It seemed dishonest to her to pretend that they didn't.

"The danger of oil spills is pretty remote, Mike," she told the reporter. "More than twenty-six thousand wells have been drilled in offshore waters. Out of those there have been only four major spills. Just one of these resulted in oil reaching shore in measurable quantities."

"But they do happen."

Holly could feel Sid Hohlman's eyes on her. "Yes," she told the reporter. "Once in a while they happen."

The manager broke in quickly, "But of course statistically speaking—"

"I'm not interested in fancy numbers," Mario Palermo interrupted. "Just the fish that are in our nets." He swept out a hand to encompass Platform Kathy and its attendant paraphernalia. "All of these—these machines. They're bound to have some effect on our catch."

"Well, actually—"

Hohlman was off again on a statistical lecture which lasted until they reached the foot of the stairs leading up to the helideck. Finally winding down, he pulled Holly aside as the two visitors started up to the pad.

"I didn't appreciate that little stunt you pulled earlier, Holly," he told her stiffly. "Or the way you all but called me a liar a few minutes ago." He turned, smiled and held up an I'll-be-with-you-in-a-minute hand to the others. When his hand dropped, he let it rest casually on her shoulder. Good lord, Holly thought. Not again!

"As a matter of fact," Hohlman went on, "I haven't been at all pleased with your attitude lately. I think it's time we discussed the matter."

His hand felt like a lead weight on her arm, and Holly couldn't help contrasting it to Kirk Roberts's touch. "What do you have in mind, Mr. Hohlman?"

The manager turned his body slightly so that he faced away from the others. "You're off duty the day after tomorrow, aren't you?"

Holly nodded tersely. She had a pretty good idea where the conversation was leading.

"That might be a very good time for us to get together. Actually, I thought you might come over to my apartment for dinner one night. It would be quiet there—we should be able to talk undisturbed."

His hand was making its way across her shoulders as he spoke and it was all Holly could do not to kick him again. She'd be willing to bet next month's paycheck on how much talking they'd do.

"Well, my dear? What do you say?"

"I say take your hand off my shoulder." Holly knew the risk she was taking. Rebuffing one's boss twice in one day did not make for good job security. She also knew that if she had to feel that hand of his for one more minute she'd scream!

Hohlman leaned forward as if he hadn't heard her clearly. "Perhaps you didn't understand what I said, my dear. You see I—"

"You heard the lady, Hohlman. Take your hand off her shoulder!"

Holly whirled to find Kirk Roberts. "What are you doing here? I don't remember calling out the Marines."

Kirk eyed Hohlman's arm, which was draped over her shoulder. "Maybe you should have. You look as if you're about to be taken captive by the enemy."

"See here, Roberts," Hohlman broke in, keeping his hand firmly entrenched where it was. "This is a private conversation. There's no need for you to—"

"The lady said move your hand, Hohlman. I suggest you do it. Now!"

Holly looked nervously toward the visitors, who were watching the drama curiously from the helideck. "Kirk, let go of him," she told the diver tersely. "I can handle this myself."

Holly was unsure what happened next. There was a blur of movement as an arm streaked out of nowhere toward Sid Hohlman's hand. She heard her boss's cry of surprise, then suddenly the weight was no longer on her shoulder.

Holly jerked backwards at the unexpected release, tripping in her unbalanced state on some pipes that were laid across the deck. Blindly she reached out for support, unknowingly letting her hand come to rest on the mud hose which fed the stream of drilling fluid down the drill stem.

Carl Morris's cry of warning came too late. Holly lurched and fell sideways, the force of her weight causing the mud hose to disconnect from the swivel and send a stream of thick black fluid shooting into the air.

When the stream of mud hit her it was as if in a dream. Beside her she heard a muffled cry, and her peripheral vision picked up a flurry of hands and legs. She was only marginally aware of a series of quick, blinding flashes and the scattered laughs of some of the crew. Lifting her head, she was horrified to see a pair of furious, bulbous eyes glaring out at her from beneath a sea of mud.

It was Sid Hohlman's cry which had pierced her consciousness, his splendidly tailored arms and legs which had protested the gooey downpour. He lay next to her on his back like a frustrated beetle, all howls and expletives, limbs clawing futilely at the air.

She had drenched her boss. Of all the people in the world, she had just buried Worldwide's regional manager under ten pounds of sludgy, slimy mud!

Squeezing her eyes shut, she lowered her head back onto the deck. Never let it be said that Holly Marie Bishop did not do these things up in style. With a little groan, she wondered if West Coast Oil was accepting job applications this week!

2

I figure that with unemployment I can last until Christmas—along with a little belt tightening and lots of beans."

Holly and Carl Morris had finished eating dinner and were sitting in the crew's dining room sipping coffee and eating hot pie à la mode. Most of the day crew had already left the cafeteria, and the two were enjoying a moment of relative quiet.

"Come on, it was an accident. How do you know Hohlman's going to take it out on you?" Carl took a large bite of steaming pie and home-made ice cream and sighed in satisfaction as the confection hit his mouth.

Holly took a bite of her own dessert. "How do you know we're going to hit oil on the number five well? I suppose there's a chance we may not, but only a fool would bet against it."

"Hohlman did look upset," Carl said, polishing off the rest of his dessert.

"Upset? When he finally got up from the deck he looked like the Loch Ness monster rising from the deep." She eyed him in annoyance. "And I wish you wouldn't look as if you found the whole episode so funny."

"It *was* funny. Doggone it, Holly, seeing Sid Hohlman rolling around the mud in that three-piece suit of his was the best thing to happen on this rig all week. Correction, make that all year."

"For the rest of you maybe," she said dryly. "Remember, yours truly was rolling around down there with him—not my favorite mud wrestling partner, I might add. It took me nearly an hour to scrub all that dirt out of my hair and clothes."

Carl chuckled. "Just think how long it's going to take Hohlman to get it out of his fancy three-hundred-dollar suit." He looked delighted by the idea. "I tell you, honey, that little mud bath did more for the crew's morale then all the cook's desserts put together."

"Wonderful. The next time things get a little dull out here I'll know how to liven them up."

Carl laughed. "Honey, you liven up this rig just by being here. You're worth two Sid Hohlmans at twice the price."

Holly reached across the table for the toolpusher's hand. "Thanks, Carl. That means a lot to me. It's good to know I've got you—" her attention wandered as four latecomers walked into the dining room—"on my side."

Holly was no longer looking at Carl and he had to lean forward to catch her last words. Following her gaze, he saw Kirk Roberts and his three-man diving crew moving through the serving line.

"You could just as easily blame that guy for what happened," Carl told her. "Although personally, I'd rather award him a medal."

Holly watched Kirk lead the men to a table on the far side of the room. They were deep in conversation, and Holly guessed that they were mapping out tomorrow's diving operation. "His crew must have arrived this afternoon with the supply ship."

Carl nodded. "Along with all their equipment, which is considerable. That one—" he motioned to the dark haired man sitting next to Kirk—"is Butch Kelley. He and Roberts were UDT's in Vietnam. The two younger ones, Larry Rees and Don Cassill, are Santa Barbara J.C. diving graduates. They've been with Roberts for about three or four years now."

By UDT, Holly knew that Kirk Roberts and Butch Kelley had been part of an underwater demolition team during the Vietnam conflict. "I've heard they're pretty good."

"Best in the business. Although I'm surprised Roberts hasn't quit by now. Commercial diving's a young man's game." Carl sipped his coffee. "At his age every dive he takes could be his last. It's a wonder he's made it this long."

"How old is Roberts, anyway? If he was in 'Nam he must be—"

"Thirty-eight. According to company records," Carl filled in. "Roughly five to eight years older then he should be to do that kind of work."

"He doesn't look it." She studied him with interest. Despite Roberts's earnest expression, he didn't look much older than the young Cal Poly Tech men who

31

wind-sailed off Morro Bay. There wasn't a spare inch of fat on that muscled body. "He seems to be in good shape," she told Carl.

"He has to be to make his living as a commercial diver. Sooner or later, though, no matter how physically fit you are, that business is going to take its toll. It isn't rated one of the world's most hazardous occupations without damn good reason."

"From what I've heard, they don't exactly go out of their way to take the easy road, either."

"You heard right. Roberts and his crew will take on just about any job, no matter how dangerous it is. And they've got the reputation for doing it right."

"They get paid to do it right."

Carl nodded. "True. And the more risk, the more money."

Carl drained his coffee and stood, stacking his dirty plates back onto the tray. "Still," he said as they bussed their dishes and headed for the door, "there isn't enough money in the world to get me to go down there. No thanks. The old prince will stick to a nice, safe, dry platform any day!"

Once outside the cafeteria, Carl and Holly went in different directions. As usual, Carl wanted to take one more look at the drilling operation before turning in for the night. For her part, Holly decided the evening was too lovely to go inside yet, and crossing the deck, she made her way to the far corner of the platform. Because there was no air pollution to block nature, she had long since discovered that sunsets aboard offshore rigs were spectacular. Tonight was no exception. Already the sky was turning a vivid orange-red where the sun was sinking into the horizon.

Wearily, Holly leaned against the guardrail, elbows

resting on the metal bar, chin cupped in her hands. It really was beautiful, she thought, trying to trace the lines of yellow, orange and red as they flowed easily into one other. A fitting end to a remarkable day. In less than thirteen hours she had kicked her boss, drenched him with mud and met one of the most exciting men she'd ever seen in her life. Not bad for one day's work.

"Lovely, isn't it?"

The low voice came as such a surprise that Holly's hands slipped, very nearly causing her chin to bump on the guardrail. She sensed the broad shoulders behind her, the slender, tapered hips, the tan face. Kirk Roberts!

She turned to find him grinning at her. "You startled me," she told him almost accusingly. "I didn't hear you walk up behind me."

He'd enjoyed watching her unobserved. She made a striking contrast against the constant moving background of the sea, tall and proud, yet possessing a subtle vulnerability that appealed to him. "You were too busy watching nature," he told her. "How can a mere mortal compete with that?"

Too damn well, Holly thought. Aloud, she said, "This is the part of the day I enjoy most on Kathy. I never get tired of the sunsets."

Kirk joined her in looking at the brilliantly colored horizon. "I know what you mean. It's beautiful." But his eyes were no longer on the setting sun. Holly caught her breath as he brushed his fingers through the rich dark hair she'd allowed to flow freely about her shoulders this evening. "You got it all out."

"Out?"

"The mud. From this afternoon."

"The mud! Of course. Yes—I finally got it out."

Then she remembered how it got there in the first place. "What made you grab Mr. Hohlman's arm like that?"

"Why not? He was grabbing your shoulder. It seemed like a fair exchange."

"That exchange resulted in one heck of a mess." She noticed he was wearing a tightly woven knit shirt tonight. It clung in a distracting way to his upper body, outlining the muscles in his neck and shoulders. A little transmitter in her brain began to emit warning signals. Tread carefully Holly. This man has proven himself to be dangerous. "You should have stayed out of it," she told him. "I had the situation under control."

"Oh?" She was irritated to see the sea-blue eyes laughing at her. "Then I'd hate to be around when things get out of control. Hohlman looked as if he was about to devour you whole."

"Sid Hohlman's bark is always worse than his bite. If you hadn't come down on us like gangbusters, I would simply have refused to have dinner with him and that would have been the end of it." She looked at him in annoyance. "Now he's got one heck of a cleaning bill and my job security is worth about five cents on the open market."

He looked at her through the rapidly falling dusk. The rosy glow of the sunset softly lit her face, and she seemed more lovely than ever. "You really enjoy your job, don't you? But why an offshore drilling engineer?"

The question surprised her. Not because it was unusual—after five years with Worldwide Oil Holly was used to being asked about her unique career—but because he really seemed to care about the answer.

"I suppose one reason is because I've always loved the water," she told him. "No one spends fifteen years in competitive swimming unless they either like the sport or derive masochistic pleasure from looking like a stewed prune." She hesitated for a moment, looking out at the soft mauve horizon which was all that was left of the blazing sunset. "Or I suppose I could just as easily blame my mother," she went on. "She teaches math and science at Gilroy High School, in a little town south of San Jose where I grew up. While other kids played hide-and-seek, I was tackling logarithms and the thornier aspects of π^2." She grinned up at Kirk sheepishly, afraid she might be boring him. "Exciting, huh?"

"It's an interesting combination." He didn't look bored. "How did swimming get into the act?"

"Dad has to take the blame for that. He teaches P.E. at the same high school as Mom," she explained. "By the time I was seven he was so worried by my lack of exercise that in desperation he introduced me to the school's swimming pool."

"And you liked it."

"I loved it. It was a completely different world for me. From then on when I wasn't calculating the uneven side of an isosceles triangle I was working out with the local swim team and competing in every meet I could find."

"And by the time you graduated from Gilroy High you'd decided to become an oil engineer."

"Not quite, but close. I got a civil engineering scholarship to Stanford University. From there it wasn't too big a jump to what I'm doing now."

"And your swimming?"

"Equal time, of course. I had to keep Dad happy." He laughed and Holly eyed him curiously. "What about you?" she asked. "What made you decide to become a commercial diver?"

Kirk shrugged. "Oh, I don't know. I stumbled into it during 'Nam and it seemed natural enough to go on with it afterwards."

"And before that?"

"High school—college—the usual." He seemed purposefully vague, and Holly wondered why. Then he reached out a hand and brushed an unruly strand of hair from her face, and it suddenly seemed unimportant. "Did you know you have beautiful hair?" he asked softly.

Holly swallowed. She wondered if he realized that the hand he'd left resting so casually on her shoulder was about to burn a hole through her jacket? Regroup battle defenses, her inner voice warned. She'd let a few minutes casual conversation lull her into a false sense of security. Emergency measures were in order.

Holly smiled up at him and said lightly, "Well, it's about that time, isn't it? It's been nice talking to you, but I've got another five A.M. call tomorrow morning so I'll just—"

She hadn't reckoned on reflexes honed sharp over fifteen years of underwater service. Skillfully he utilized her movement away from the guardrail to propel her into his arms. One of his hands circled her waist, the other left her shoulder to gently cup and raise her chin. "You have beautiful lips, too," he whispered. "In fact, you're a very lovely lady."

Despite a sudden restriction in her throat, she managed to say, "And you have a line as smooth as a water slide. But I'm just not interested in a platform romance."

The heightened beat of her heart belied her words. "Oh, no? We'll see about that."

After that Holly had no breath left to speak. She

knew he was going to kiss her, yet her body simply wouldn't move. While one tiny, intact portion of her brain bravely sounded the alarm, the rest of her mind became distracted with the way his hands were moving across the small of her back, and the erratic way the nerve endings in that particular portion of her anatomy were beginning to react. The attack posed a grave threat to her defense system, and Holly could only moan helplessly as she succumbed to the invasion.

He kissed her just as the last faint glow disappeared from the western sky. At first his touch was tentative, and she almost felt a twinge of disappointment. After this morning she had expected—good lord, what *had* she expected? Surely not to be kissing him again!

Yet here she stood, on the western-most corner of Platform Kathy, surrounded by men, equipment and noise, held tightly in the arms of a man she'd met only that morning. Dementia. Absolute, unmitigated dementia!

Then all thoughts were obliterated as Kirk's hand gently slid beneath her blue-cord jacket to trace a fiery line along her collarbone. When she shivered from the contact, he kissed her more intensely, coaxing her lips apart to probe inside her mouth with the tip of his inquisitive tongue.

Holly could feel the roar of her own blood in her ears as he molded her against him. She had never reacted like this to a man before. Vaguely she wondered why it was happening now.

"You know this is crazy, don't you?" she mumbled as his lips moved to the hollow of her throat. "What if somebody sees us?" Through a growing haze of desire, Holly was struck by the incongruity of her words. Not, "Why are you doing this to me?" or "Why am I letting you?" But of all things, "What if somebody sees us?" Could there be any further doubt as to her sanity?

Then his mouth returned to her lips and she could only think that if this was insanity, then it had a lot to recommend it. Waves of pleasure washed over her as his hand traveled adeptly over the soft fabric of her shirt.

Then the hand beneath her jacket moved lower, and Holly shuddered as it lightly traced the full swell of her breasts. She felt her nipples harden beneath the flannel lining of her sweat shirt. The shock of this reaction brought reality crashing back.

"Kirk—stop. I don't want to do this!" Sounds of the night crew were penetrating the sensual fog which had settled around her. Fighting these heady sensations, Holly pushed hard against his chest in an effort to break the spell. "This is crazy. Someone's bound to see us."

His breath feathered lightly across her lips and she had to resist the urge to reach out and recapture his mouth. Distance, Holly. Whatever it takes—get some distance!

But there was no need to press further. Slowly Kirk released her, then leaned back against the guardrail where he regarded her with a lazy grin. "Did I forget to tell you that you kiss beautifully, too?" he said with unbelievable aplomb.

Holly was temporarily at a loss for words, his imperturbability rendering her speechless. Then, catching the amusement in his eyes, she snapped, "You may be used to women falling all over you, Mr. Roberts, but you've picked on the wrong woman this time." She glared at him through the growing darkness, the lights from the deck only partially illuminating the far corner of the rig where they were standing. "Believe it or not, I didn't get out of the frying pan this morning just to fall right back into the fire tonight. I don't know what you expect from me—" all right, she had a pretty good idea— "but the last thing I need in my life right now is a platform romance."

The muscles around his mouth twitched and even through the gloom she could see his eyes light with mischief. "Does that mean it's all over between us?"

"Over?" She stared at him in disbelief. "How can something be over that hasn't even begun?"

"Good point. When can we begin?"

"You're crazy, did you know that? All that water must have gone to your head." Holly slipped past him and started for the stairs to the crew's quarters.

She could hear a note of laughter in the voice that followed her. "Pleasant dreams. See you in the morning."

And because they were stuck together on a twelve-thousand-ton rig twenty miles off the coast of California, she knew that he would!

Holly squinted at the early morning sun and examined the mud which clung in messy globs to the drill stem. Deftly, she reached out and collected a sample to take below to test in her lab. She rubbed a small amount of the black substance between her fingers and decided it was probably time to add a slightly different combination of chemicals to the water and clay now that the new bit had been attached.

At the end of the deck she could see Kirk Roberts suiting up for his first dive aboard Kathy. He had paired up with Larry Rees, one of the younger divers, to make the initial inspection of the rig before planning any actual repairs. And although she was a bare fifty feet aft of the deck decompression chamber, she had been doing her best all morning to pretend it didn't exist.

After last night, Holly had every intention of staying as far away from Kirk Roberts as possible. Granted, in such a confined space, avoiding a fellow crewman wasn't easy. But the alternative gave Holly ample incentive to go to whatever lengths were necessary.

Still, she could not prevent her eyes from straying occasionally in his direction. She knew that for today's initial inspection, the men would do a half-hour "bounce" dive, that is they would descend by diving bell some three hundred feet to the ocean's floor, then after thirty minutes, ascend once more in the bell to the platform decompression chamber. At that point the bell would be hooked onto the on-deck chamber, and the men would enter the decompression room without having to set foot outside. For their thirty minutes below, they would spend at least eight hours in the chamber. Holly shook her head. It seemed a heavy price to pay to have a quick look at the platform's tangled steel understructure.

She saw that both men were wearing neoprene wet suits and carried a two-tank supply of special air mixture strapped to their backs. During their time below, Holly knew they would be in constant voice communication with Butch Kelley, who as second in command, would monitor the dive from the surface. Neither Kirk nor Larry had put on their helmets as yet, and Holly could see the hard lines of concentration on Roberts's face. Flippant as he was out of the water, it was obvious he took his work seriously. But then, to have survived this long in such a hazardous business, he'd have to.

While she looked on, the divers pulled on their helmets and adjusted the breathing valves. Again they paused for another series of tests, then entered the diving bell which would carry them beneath the ocean's surface. By means of a cable and winch, one of the rig's huge cranes swung the bell over the side. For several long minutes it hung suspended a hundred feet over the water, then finally, began its slow, occasionally jerky journey to the sea.

When she could no longer see the bell below the surface of the water, Holly turned back to her work. Briefly she wondered what divers thought of as they made the rapid descent through all those fathoms of water. It was certainly no place for the fainthearted, she thought fervently. Anyone who did that kind of work for a living was a breed apart!

It was some time later that Holly became aware of an unusual level of activity taking place by the deck decompression chamber. Looking over, she saw Butch Kelley talking earnestly over the diver communication system, while Don Cassill, the youngest member of the team, watched him with obvious concern.

Holly's heart bounded into her throat. Something was wrong. Something had happened to the divers!

Dropping the samples of shale she had been collecting, she hurried through the maze of equipment that separated her from the chamber. Not bothering with a small group of men who had gathered around the surface equipment, she went directly to Butch Kelley.

"What's wrong?" she asked him. "What's going on down there?"

Despite a superficial appearance of calm, the diver's eyes betrayed the first stirrings of concern. "It's nothing to get excited about," he told her, raising his face from the receiver. "The divers got temporarily separated and—"

"What do you mean they got separated?" she broke in. "You mean they're lost?"

When he hesitated, Don Cassill told her, "Larry went and got himself tangled up with a stingray. When the fish attacked he panicked and swam too far away from the bell. Kirk's down there now trying to find him."

Holly thought of the handsome, animated young man she'd watched suiting up a little more than half an hour ago. The thought of his lying somewhere down there injured made her blood run cold.

She looked at her watch, surprised to find that so much time had elapsed since the dive originated. "They've been down there nearly forty minutes. How much air do they have left?" This time she addressed the question directly to Don.

"Five, maybe ten more minutes. Depends on how much energy they expend."

Holly was about to ask another question when the sound of a voice on the other end of the communication line made her stop. Neither she nor Don Cassill moved while Butch Kelley listened to the message.

"He's found him. Rees has a bad laceration on his right thigh so it's going to be tricky getting him back to the bell."

"Will they have enough air?" She knew that hauling another diver, even in an underwater situation, used up far more air mixture than would normally be consumed. Add to that the fact that the second diver was wounded. . . . She didn't want to calculate the odds.

"It'll be close, but Kirk will make sure they have

enough." For the first time, the diver turned and really looked at Holly. "The kid's in good hands, lady. If anyone can bring him up, Roberts can."

There was a crackle of static and Kelley grabbed at the receiver. "He's got him back," he told the growing crowd. "They're in the bell." He turned to the crane operator. "Okay, Lou, haul 'em up."

Holly moved back out of the way as the crew worked quickly to bring the bell back up. She saw the rig's medical crew standing by, and almost everyone else on the platform who could leave his job temporarily to watch the drama.

There was a rousing cheer when the bell came bobbing above the surface of the water, and a dozen pairs of hands reached out to help attach it to the decompression chamber. Because the divers had to remain pressurized, all medical treatment would have to take place inside the chamber. Fully organized and ready to act, the first-aid team lost no time entering the capsule. There was nothing for the rest of them to do now but wait.

A somber hush settled over the deck as they stood by the decompression capsule. Some of the crew spoke quietly in small groups, and several men were gathered around the port holes which lined the chamber, trying to see what was going on inside.

Holly waited in a kind of dazed fear. She knew how much damage a stingray could inflict with its spikelike spines. And she knew how physically damaging it could be to undertake strenuous activity without sufficient oxygen. Butch Kelley had assumed that her primary concern had been for Larry Rees. But was it? As the long minutes ticked by, Holly stood by the chamber and wondered.

Fifteen minutes later word came out that both men

were going to be all right. Larry Rees had suffered a bad cut just above his right kneecap, but now that it had been sterilized and bound, it should begin to heal normally. Barring complications he should be back to work in about a week.

News about Kirk was even more optimistic. The diver was tired, which was understandable under the circumstances, but had sustained no lasting ill effects from his efforts with his injured diving buddy. Both men were resting now, and would remain in the decompression chamber until their bodies returned to normal surface pressure—a time which had now been extended to ten hours to compensate for their additional minutes on the bottom.

Holly walked back to her work, numb with relief. She returned Carl Morris's smile and knew that he, along with all the others on board Kathy, had been pulling for the divers below. There'd been good reason for her fears, she told herself. The divers had been in real danger and it had been perfectly natural for her to worry.

Nonetheless, Holly bypassed the drilling operation and headed for the canteen. She knew she needed some time alone before going back to work. When she poured coffee from the pot, however, she was unhappy to see that her hands were still shaking.

Not good, she told herself firmly. Not good at all.

Holly sat down and examined the situation objectively. There was no sense trying to kid herself. All rationalization aside, she knew that the fear she had just experienced went far beyond what might be expected for a fellow crew mate. Why, she wondered?

Holly thought about that question for a long time as she sat and drank her coffee.

3

Going to the Harbor Aquarium always felt like coming home. Even before Holly reached the old stucco building, perched like some ancient marine sentinel at the end of the Embarcadero, she felt the tensions of the past seven days loosening their hold on her body. Opening the door, she inhaled deeply of the cool, distinctly fishy air. It was good to be back.

"There you are," a loud voice greeted her from inside. "The coffee's fresh and Minxie missed you. Why don't you grab us each a cup before you check on him?"

Josie Hanson, tall, thin and in her early forties, was perched on a high stool behind the cash register. Wearing a sleeveless, halter-top dress in a bright Hawaiian print, the woman added a bold splash of color to the room.

Holly chuckled, grabbed her friend's cup from the counter and walked through the cluttered aquarium gift shop into an even more cluttered room in the back. Pulling a mug from a hook behind the automatic coffee machine, she filled both cups, then headed back into the shop.

"And how, please tell, does a sea lion go about missing someone?" she asked, handing Josie the steaming mug and sinking into an armless desk chair behind the counter. Lunch-hour business was always slow at the gift shop, and Holly knew it would be several minutes before the afternoon wave of customers descended.

"With a hell of a lot of bleats, barks and two of the biggest, saddest brown eyes that ever ogled a fish."

"Have you checked his wound?" Minxie, a young California sea lion, had been brought in two weeks ago after having been attacked by a shark in the offshore waters. Because of the pup's puggish face and playful antics, Holly had dubbed him Minxie.

Josie lit a cigarette. "It's coming along okay. If he'd quit rubbing it against the side of the pen, it would be a lot better. Not very bright, your noisy little friend." Josie regarded Holly over the rim of her mug. "How about you? What's new on that floating gas station of yours? Hit any new geysers this week?"

"It's gushers, and no, number five hasn't come in yet." Holly smiled at her friend. "And we take precautions to control the gushing these days. Can't afford the waste."

Josie gestured shortly with the beringed hand holding the cigarette. "Whatever. With all those men out there I don't see how you can concentrate on oil anyway."

"Not you, too!" Holly's position as Platform Kathy's sole female resident seemed to present no end of romantic possibilities to Morro Bay's more fertile minds. She wished the gossip mongers could spend one day aboard the rig and find out how romantic it really was!

Josie grinned mischievously. "Come on, Holly. Some of those guys are real knockouts."

Holly tried to ignore the flush which was creeping into her cheeks. "On the rig it's job performance that counts, not looks."

Josie leaned forward on the stool, a slow smile spreading across her face. "By God, Holly Bishop, you're blushing! There is someone, isn't there? And he must be nothing short of gorgeous to have gotten through that lead shield of yours."

Holly moaned. From past experience she knew denial would be useless. When Josie zeroed in on a target, she did it with all the accuracy of a guided missile. "All right, I give up, although for the record I'm not so much attracted as overwhelmed by the man. His name's Kirk Roberts and his diving company's doing our quarterly platform inspection."

"And—?"

Holly shook her head helplessly. "All right, he's gorgeous. He's thirty-eight, very tall, blond and built like a linebacker for the Los Angeles Rams. Now, is there anything else you'd like to know?"

Josie grinned broadly. "Yes. Does he come equipped with a brother? Preferably older? Although heck, I'm not fussy. There's a lot to be said for younger men, too."

"And what about Pete?" Josie and Pete Zinsser, manager of the Tidewater seafood restaurant next door, had been a steady item in Morro Bay long before Holly came on the scene. Thrice divorced,

Josie had recently been displaying unmistakable signs of matrimonial intent.

The older woman shrugged and put out her cigarette. "Pete's understanding. That's one of his better points."

"No man's that understanding. Besides, I don't expect to be talking that much to Mr. Roberts."

"You're kidding, of course." Josie looked at her friend as if she'd taken one giant step toward insanity. "A man like that doesn't come walking into your life every day."

"He walked onto the rig, Josie, not into my life. Divers come and go everyday. When Kirk Roberts finishes on Kathy he'll be off again for parts unknown."

"Then for heaven's sake enjoy him while he's here. You can live off the memories for years."

Holly finished her coffee and rose, just as the first customer of the afternoon came through the gift shop door. "No thanks, Josie, some memories I can live without. There's enough talk as it is about my being the only woman out there. I've never dated a fellow crew member yet and I have no intentions of starting now. I don't care how gorgeous he is."

Holly found Ginny Palermo scraping algae off the sides of an empty tank in the aquarium behind the gift shop. At least she found a slim derierre and two slender, shorts-clad legs standing atop a ladder. But those were distinctive enough to announce whose upper half was hidden in the cement-backed tank.

Holly tapped gently on the glass. "Anybody home?"

A pretty young face popped out of the tank. "Hi. Boy, am I glad to see you. I was beginning to get dizzy in there. Now I've got an excuse for a break."

"I'm glad I'm good for something." Holly peered into the tank's empty interior. "What's going in here?"

"Josie's new Longhorn Sculpin arrived this morning. She's so happy with it, she's decided to dedicate this whole side of the room to North American shore fish."

"Sounds like our Josie. Never let it be said she let a little thing like space and money stand in the way of scientific expansion." She leaned comfortably against the side of the tank and eyed her young friend. Ginny's long dark hair was pulled back into a ponytail today. That, plus smudges of dirt on the tip of her small nose, made her look more like twelve then seventeen. "All ready for graduation?"

Ginny hopped down from the ladder. "Mom's been ready for weeks," she said with a wry face. "She's planning a big family celebration. You know, ten pasta dishes, ham, turkey, cake, ice cream and enough Chianti to launch every boat in Pop's fishing fleet. There'll be relatives there I haven't seen in years—if ever."

"Hey, don't look a gift horse in the mouth. If I was graduating with a four-point-oh grade-point-average I'd expect the President to declare a national holiday. You'll be the first Palermo in your family to go on to college, won't you?"

"If I ever get there." The girl sighed and leaned next to her friend against the tank. "Mom and Pop won't even discuss my future."

"Same problem, huh?"

Ginny nodded. "Pop says being a drilling engineer is totally out of the question. He makes it sound as if I'm planning a major act of treason. And Mom—well, she always goes along with what Pop says. Talk about unreasonable."

Holly smiled at the girl. "Being reasonable is a matter of viewpoint sometimes. To your parents, you're the one who's being unreasonable. I know it sounds corny, but they only want what's best for you."

"Sure. As long as it doesn't go against the precious Palermo family tradition."

Ginny made no effort to mask her bitterness, and Holly could well imagine the fisherman's reaction to his daughter's plans to become a petroleum engineer. Guiltily she wondered how much Ginny's admiration for her had led to that decision.

"I thought once he met you and saw the rig he'd change his mind," Ginny went on. "But if anything, it's worse now. I think he found all that machinery intimidating. He's convinced it has to have a bad effect on the fish."

"An oil platform can be pretty overpowering. It takes time to get used to."

"But that's just it," Ginny cried. "Time's running out. It's nearly June and fall semester starts in September. If I can't change their minds soon it'll be too late to register."

Holly put her arm around the girl's shoulders and gave her a sympathetic squeeze. "I know it's hard, honey, but try to be patient. This isn't easy for your parents, either."

Even as she said the words, Holly realized how empty they sounded. Patience was hard enough to practice at twenty-seven. At seventeen, it was about as easy as trying to pretend boys didn't exist.

Holly muttered several more platitudes, berated herself for only making the situation worse and finally decided Ginny was better off working out her frustrations on the fish tank. Leaving the girl scrubbing away, she walked outside where a row of outdoor enclosures accommodated the aquarium's seal population. A loud bark heralded her arrival.

"You sure make a lot of noise for one small sea lion," she told Minxie. "But it's nice to be missed. Yes, yes," she cooed, holding out a fish to the eager pup. "I missed you, too."

Carefully, Holly examined Minxie's wound. "Now why do you rub it against the wall like that, huh?" she asked the playful sea lion, patting his head affectionately. "You really are a minx. Did you know that?"

Unabashed by the gentle criticism, Minxie barked loudly and flopped with a splash into the water, where he performed several enthusiastic flips as if to prove his good health. With an expression very close to an open-mouthed grin, he hopped back onto the wall, leaned back and clapped his front flippers, obviously well pleased with his performance.

Holly laughed. "You ought to be in a circus," she told him, throwing the pup another small fish. "You're a born ham."

She spent several more minutes with Minxie, then finished her round of the aquarium, renewing old acquaintances and meeting the new fish and sea mammals which had made their way into the world or out of the sea since her last visit.

At three, Holly called it a day and left the aquarium to walk three-quarters of a mile south to a small beach she'd discovered early in her stay in Morro Bay. Because it was surrounded on three sides by a grove of eucalyptus trees and a dense growth of brush lupia, she could usually count on the tiny clearing being deserted. She spread out her towel, then peeled off the shirt and jeans she'd worn over her tiny rust-colored bikini. After one long, luxurious stretch toward the sun, she headed for the water.

"Mercy," Holly muttered, shivering as her legs took the impact of the first chilly wave. Taking a deep breath, she plunged into the surf and struck out from shore with sure, powerful strokes. As soon as her muscles loosened, she settled into a measured but steady pace, swimming back and forth in quarter-mile laps parallel to the beach. After twenty minutes, she turned on her back and floated, arms and legs dangling easily on the surface of the brisk water. Above, the sun blazed, its rays warming her like some giant electric blanket. Below, the cool sea massaged every tired, aching muscle. Holly closed her eyes. Heavenly!

The pull on her leg came as such a shock that Holly gasped, swallowing a mouthful of salty water as she struggled against the steel-hard grip. She kicked out blindly, having no clear idea where she should aim, striking out instinctively toward the low, laughing voice at her feet.

"Take it easy," the voice said. "Stop kicking and I'll let you go."

Holly gave one strong push with her legs and floated free of his grasp. There was no mistaking that voice. Kirk Roberts!

"What are . . . what are you doing here?" she sputtered. Salt water burned at her throat, making it difficult to speak. He was about four feet away from her, wet blond hair plastered against his finely chiseled face, aquamarine eyes following her with maddening enjoyment. "What the hell do you mean, grabbing at me like that? I . . . I could have drowned."

In two easy strokes he was beside her. Just below the surface of the water he could see glimpses of creamy shoulders and soft, rounded cleavage. "It would take more than that to drown you," he said. "I've been watching you for the past ten minutes. You swim like a fish."

She looked at him in amazement. "How in the world did you find me . . . or this beach?"

"Josie told me. Wait," he laughed. "Before you ask me how I knew about Josie's aquarium, I talked to Carl Morris this morning. He said you spend a lot of time there during your seven-off."

"But why go to so much trouble to find me?"

His face creased in a frank grin and Holly felt the familiar prickles on the back of her neck. "Would you believe I've got a thing for beautiful lady engineers who specialize in one hundred-meter freestyle and do differential equations for a hobby?"

"Kirk, be serious."

"Never," he replied lightly. Suddenly he wanted to see more of her than the rippling water would allow. Kirk nodded toward the shore. "Come on, I'll race you in."

Holly held nothing back in their dash back to the beach, but despite her fifteen years of competitive training, Kirk touched land more than a full body length before she did.

"Hey, you *are* good," he told her as they lay catching their breath on the sand. "You made me work for every inch."

Holly pulled a wet strand of auburn hair from her eyes and mouth. "I'm out of practice. You won by virtue of superior brawn."

"Thanks a lot. Do you always concede so gracefully?"

"Only when I lose."

She turned on her side and looked at him with open

curiosity. His body, naked except for the small, navy blue triangle of his swim trunks, was magnificent, just as she'd imagined it would be. His shoulders were very broad and muscular, his arms rippling with the strength acquired from long years as a commercial diver.

His face seemed carved from the finest stone, the valleys and plains sharply defined yet softened by a sensitivity she hadn't noticed before. Two small scars, one above the right eyebrow, and one just below the line of his chin, marred his otherwise evenly tanned good looks. But Holly decided they added rather than subtracted to the overall effect, giving his face a kind of vulnerability she found appealing.

His skin gleamed with moisture, matting the fine, blond hair which covered his trim body. His swimsuit clung to his hips, and her eyes followed the line of golden down which grew darker as it progressed toward the suit. When she reached the apex of his trunks, her breath caught in her throat.

"Well?"

The single, husky word startled Holly as much as if he'd physically touched her. She cleared her throat nervously. "Excuse me?"

His smile was an intimate, devilish caress. He had found the voyage of her eyes over his body exciting. "Do I pass inspection?"

Holly colored. "Sorry, I didn't mean to stare. I was just thinking that you look remarkably fit for a man who's—" She stopped, flustered.

"For a man pushing forty?"

"I meant it as a compliment."

He looked amused. "I know you did." To her supreme discomfort, he was examining her now just as frankly as she'd looked at him. His blue-green eyes traveled from her shoulders to her slim waist, to the gentle swell of her buttocks and down her long suntanned legs.

"You're not bad yourself," he told her with a lazy, sexy grin. "For a woman pushing thirty, that is."

"Ouch. I guess I deserved that."

To her surprise, Kirk reached over and brushed his lips lightly over her mouth. "You deserve to be soundly kissed. You know I'm almost glad Larry's on the mend for a couple of days. It gives us time to get to know each other better."

"How . . . how is Larry?" she asked hoarsely. Was that really her voice? All that sea water must have affected her vocal chords more than she'd realized. Surely he didn't have to sit so close to her. The beach wasn't *that* small! "I . . . ah, I heard the cut on his leg was pretty serious."

"It was, but it was attended to promptly. He'll be fine in a day or two. In the meantime—"

The unfinished words hung between them like an invisible cord drawing them together. Holly felt herself melting into those wonderful sea-blue eyes, almost feeling the provocative curve of those lips. "Will it take you long to get started?"

Only when she saw the slow grin spreading over his face did Holly realize the double meaning in her words. "With the platform, of course."

He nodded seriously. "Of course." He seemed to give the question careful consideration. "Well, I wasn't down there long enough for a full inspection, but it looks like the structure itself needs a fair amount of work. And I noticed at least one anode that's working itself loose. It'll take six, maybe eight weeks to finish."

The anodes were the positively charged electrodes placed below the rig to attract erosion away from the understructure itself. Periodic replacement of these formed an important part of the divers' quarterly maintenance work.

"And after that . . . you're off to where?" Holly wondered why it was so difficult to ask such a simple question. She knew he would move on. She had told Josie he would move on. So why did it bother her so damn much that he *would* move on?

He shrugged lightly but he had noticed her slight hesitation. "Oh, I don't know. We've had offers to go back to the North Sea. There've been feelers from Egypt, Brazil, Spain and Indonesia, too. Take your pick."

Holly went along with the game, glad to keep the conversation on a casual footing. "Egypt, of course. I've always wanted to see the Pyramids."

"What about Spain? We could take in the bull-fights."

"Uh–uh. Too bloody."

"There's always *Jai alai* in the Basque country."

"There's a thought." She frowned. "But I don't know a thing about the game."

"It's easy to learn. The betting's a little tricky. Anyone with your knack for numbers, though, ought to master it in no time."

"We could make our fortune."

Grinning, he said, "And drill our own wells."

"And travel all over the world in our own private jet."

"With long black limousines waiting for us at every airport." They were laughing so hard by then that it seemed natural when Kirk reached out and drew her close to his side. Holly felt the strong, masculine feel of him against her naked skin. Suddenly she was much too aware of him as a man, a very handsome, very desirable man. Her laughter subsided awkwardly and she pulled away. He didn't try to stop her.

Kirk had felt her stiffen. The moment had become too relaxed, too intimate, and she'd turned away from him, frightened, as if she had to hold herself apart. He'd sensed this same reserve aboard the platform and now he thought he understood why. "It must be difficult," he said. "Being the only woman aboard a rig."

"It is sometimes." She grinned self-consciously. "At least it's never dull."

"No, I wouldn't think so." He ran his right hand lightly over her shoulder and down her arm. He could feel the tension there, the muscles knotted beneath his fingers. "With you around I'm surprised any work gets accomplished."

"Are you accusing me of being a distraction, Mr. Roberts?" She reached out to remove his hand from her arm, but instead ended up running her fingers over his roughened skin. Even his hand had character, she thought distractedly. A dozen tiny scars hinted at untold stories and close calls that Holly didn't even want to think about. "In fact, that could be construed as a sexist remark."

"There's no doubt you're a distraction," he breathed, his hand continuing to run up and down her arm. "And if that's a sexist remark, I plead guilty as charged."

She was bombarded by conflicting sensations. She wanted him to move his hand and she wanted to kiss those magic fingertips all at the same time. He was sitting too close yet not close enough. The proximity of his lips was too threatening to her sanity and too glorious to be evaded.

Then his face lowered to hers and suddenly the only

thing that mattered was that he was going to kiss her. Vaguely she realized that further experimentation with Kirk Roberts might well prove dangerous. But then, she rationalized, what scientific advancement had ever been achieved without a certain amount of personal risk?

Holly raised her chin and met his lips halfway. She sucked in her breath as they brushed against hers, lightly at first, the barest, feathery, wisp of a touch. Very dangerous, she thought, succumbing to the marvelous, dizzying feel of him. But what a glorious way to go!

"Mmmm," he murmured into her ear. Her skin felt refreshingly cool beneath his fingers, and he didn't resist the urge to pull her tightly against him. He inhaled deeply of her, then sighed. "How can a lady who works with mud all day feel so soft and smell so sweet?"

His hands were warm and slightly rough where they massaged her waist and back. The physical contact took away Holly's breath and she felt weak when his lips again returned to her mouth. "There's nothing wrong with the way you taste, either," he whispered.

One hand tilted back her head, the other caressed her cheek, the fingertips slipping into her hair to describe soft, tingling little circles just above her ear. This time his kiss held no restraint, only a new hunger. Quickly he teased apart her lips to allow full access to the sweet honey which lay inside.

Holly had never felt so much excitement in a kiss, so much passion. It went deep as her soul, igniting the darkest, most private regions of her body. His tongue tasted and probed, exploring her mouth with an electrifying thoroughness. She felt exposed, revealed to this man in a way she'd never felt before, and the realization both terrified and thrilled her. She knew a brief moment of terror as she realized how quickly matters were getting out of control. Holly reached out to push him away. Instead, her palms treacherously remained on his chest to feel the soft hair which had dried to form a light, curly down.

His own hand brushed down her cheek and neck to the delicate line of her collar bone. While his lips continued to ravage and pleasure her mouth, the hand dipped lower to run along her shoulder and arm to the swell of her breasts. She trembled as his fingers traced a path along the top of her suit.

He could feel her confusion, and immediately set out to reassure her. "Relax," he murmured. Gently, his lips touched the corner of each eye, then the hollow of her cheeks, and finally her mouth.

Only when he felt her relax in his arms did he bring his attention back to her suit, smoothly easing the straps down her arms until the tiny bra was around her waist and he had unrestrained access to her full, high breasts. With a little moan, Kirk turned her onto her back where he towered above her like the golden god she had at first imagined him to be. The falling sun was at his back, forming a brilliant halo behind the gold of his hair, and the vision was so dazzling that Holly blinked and closed her eyes.

"No," he told her. "Look at me. I want us to see each other."

Obediently, Holly opened her eyes, and because he had shifted slightly, all that filled her vision now were the strong, expressive planes of his face and the deep longing in his eyes. She felt another shiver of fright.

"This is all wrong." What little remained of rational thought struggled to be heard above the furious pounding of her heart.

"Tell your body that," he breathed.

His head bent to capture the darkness of a nipple, his lips circling it leisurely. He moved to kiss the other breast and Holly felt the last vestige of control slipping away. With an ache that seemed to explode from the depths of her soul, she twisted beneath him, not wanting him to go on, not wanting him to stop.

Then his mouth was back on hers, but his hands continued what his lips had started, cupping and massaging her breasts until she was full of desire for him. Nothing in her past had prepared her for this driving response. She had felt desire before, even passion. But the flame which consumed her now made past experience seem tame by comparison.

His muscular chest pressed into her, flattening her breasts, taking away what little remained of her breath and sanity. She felt his hands at the elastic rim of her bikini briefs now, and she arched up and felt the hard desire growing in him. Holly moved restlessly against this hardness, desperate to feel his need for her, unable to control her own. Sensing her surrender, Kirk's hands grew bolder, dipping beneath the panties to find the soft silken essence of her femininity. She shuddered at this intimate invasion, fighting with the last tenuous threads of sanity to regain control of the situation.

"Please, Kirk. Stop. This . . . this is a mistake."

"No mistake ever felt like this." His hand moved beneath her hips, raising them against his own. She felt so good, so perfect beneath him. "I never expected to find someone like you aboard that rig, honey."

Inadvertently, Kirk had said the only words capable of bringing Holly to her senses. Her one unvarying, inviolate rule for the past five years had been not to become involved with a fellow crew member. Her very job survival depended upon this. Now, after two brief days, Kirk Roberts threatened everything she'd been working for. There was too much at stake to be sacrificed for a few fleeting moments of sexual gratification.

Holly braced her body and pushed hard against Kirk's chest with the palms of her hands until a space opened between them. "Kirk, stop! Please—"

He drew back, but his fingers remained tightly on her hips as he raised his head to stare at her. A sudden wariness was forcing its way through the still smoldering desire in his eyes.

"What do you mean, stop? Honey, what's the matter with you? All of a sudden you're stiff as a board."

Holly was fighting to catch her breath. "I can't . . . I can't do this, Kirk. No platform romances. Not with you or anyone else."

He sat up then, and she was sure that the flush on his face was caused by far more than the sun. "You're serious, aren't you?"

Holly moved back across the sand and with shaking hands, yanked her suit into place. When she spoke her voice was still unsteady. "Yes, I'm serious."

She saw the flush spread to his high cheekbones and sensed the internal battle he was waging. "Look, I'm a big girl now," she told him before he could speak. "It was as much my fault as yours that things went so far. I'll also admit—" this part was a lot harder—"that I feel a certain amount of attraction for you, but that doesn't mean I'm going to give in to it. You're not the first man on board a rig to make a pass, and I don't suppose you'll be the last. I'm not going to let any of you ruin my career."

"At a time like this you're worried about your job?"

He stared at her for a long moment, wondering if she was serious. Kirk had held enough women in his arms to know when one was responding to him. And this woman was very definitely responding.

Then his eyes crinkled into a smile as he seemed to find some humor in the situation. "I hate to disillusion you, honey, but nowadays sexual acts performed in the privacy of your own bedroom are no longer grounds for being fired."

"This beach is not my bedroom. And I'm not afraid of getting fired. Just of losing the respect of the men I work with. That's important to me."

"And if we make love you think the crew won't respect you anymore?"

When he said it, it sounded as archaic as high-button shoes and bustle dresses. "You're not a woman or you'd understand," she said lamely.

A slow grin spread across his face. "If I were a woman we wouldn't be having this discussion."

His easy attitude only seemed to spotlight her own confusion. "It's a matter of professional ethics."

To her surprise, he laughed. "Lady, what just happened between us has no more to do with ethics than a used car salesman. I can see I have a lot of educating to do."

Before she could come up with a suitable response, he stood and helped her to her feet. While she watched, he pulled on a pair of dark blue cords and slipped his arms into a light blue cotton shirt. Handing over her own clothes, he shook out her towel and rolled it into a neat cylinder while she got dressed.

"Come on," he told her cheerfully. "I'm starved."

"Wait a minute." He was leading her through the brush to the nearly hidden path. "You mean starved as in eat dinner?"

"Got it in one." He hustled her through the last of the trees and onto the path. "I thought we'd try the Tidewater, you know, the restaurant next to the aquarium. Josie says they've got terrific scampi."

"Josie says—"

"Watch your step on these rocks or you'll have one hell of a stubbed toe."

Holly lifted her feet gingerly. "Since when have you become so friendly with Josie? You just met her today and—whose car is this?" Propelled along the path by his firm arm, she had stopped at a sleek white Corvette parked to the side of the road.

"Mine—and she just recommended a restaurant, not an investment portfolio." He threw open the door. "Come on, get in."

"I am not getting in. And I'm not having dinner with you." Kirk seated her and closed the door. "Didn't you hear me?" she called out as he walked around to the driver's side. "I don't date fellow crew members."

"Fasten your seat belt. And I'm not a fellow crew member. I'm an independent diver hired by your company to make a quarterly platform inspection." He started the car. "Josie says the red snapper's good, too. It's fresh daily."

"I can't believe I'm having this conversation." Holly turned away from him, or at least as far as the seat belt, which he had finally fastened himself, would allow. "I refuse to humor you."

He turned the car back towards town. "I guess we ought to change first. Why don't I drop you off and pick you up in half an hour?"

"Why don't you drop me off, period? I'm not going to dinner."

"Or we could have the cioppino. Josie says it's a meal in itself."

Holly turned back to him. "Josie says, Josie says. How's about listening to what *Holly* says. I'm not going to have dinner with you!"

Following her directions, he pulled the car up in front of her apartment, then leaned across and opened the passenger door. "Don't be too long," he threw out as she stomped up to the entrance. "I'll be back in half an hour."

He grinned, then added, "Oh, and wear something sexy."

4

~~~~~~~~~

They dined on Scampi à la Provençale at a choice table, which obviously had not fallen to them by chance. Holly saw Josie's hand in everything from their seating to the earnest ministrations of Louis Bruchac, Tidewater's headwaiter. Pete Zinsser hovered, Louis fawned, and the pretty young cashier nearly swooned when Kirk smiled at her as they walked in. All in all it was a lovely evening—for someone who wasn't going to dinner.

"Now aren't you glad you came?" Kirk was reclining in his seat, napkin folded at the side of the empty scampi dish, blue-green eyes relaxed and looking much too amused.

"Mmmm, I guess," Holly murmured noncommittally. She was finding it difficult to remain angry after eating one of the finest shrimp dinners of her life in front of one of the most beautiful views of the

California coast. Feminine pride, however, forced her to make one more try. "You bullied me into coming."

"You were ready on time," he pointed out reasonably.

"I had to shower and change anyway."

His eyebrows rose. "Into that?"

Even Holly wasn't sure why she'd worn one of the slinkiest dresses in her closet. She had long ago decided that any woman who had to spend two weeks out of every month wearing ill-fitting men's work clothes deserved something better for her off hours. Nonetheless, she realized she was probably extravagant when it came to her private wardrobe. Delicate, lacy lingerie were her special passion, although every outfit she owned was calculated to point out that even though she was a drilling engineer, she was also a woman.

The dress she'd chosen tonight was a rich burnt sienna color that nearly matched the highlights in her hair. The soft chiffon was cut very low beneath thin straps, the fitted bodice emphasizing her tiny waist and the full, proud thrust of her breasts. Kirk's open admiration when he'd arrived at her door promptly half an hour after he'd left her, was evidence enough of what he thought of the outfit.

"I enjoy dressing up when I get a chance," Holly said, not knowing herself why she'd gone to so much trouble for a man she professed she didn't want to see.

"It's a good thing you can't go out on the rig looking like that or Worldwide's accident rate would triple." Kirk was finding it difficult to remember that this soft, utterly feminine woman sitting across from him was mud engineer aboard the platform. The dress she'd worn tonight nearly took his breath away, and he was waging a mostly losing battle trying to keep his eyes off the low, graceful sweep of the neckline. He touched her hand. "When I first saw you I had an irresistible urge to strip off those awful clothes you were wearing and see what treasures I could uncover."

Kirk's smile brought a soft flush to her cheeks. "This afternoon on the beach, I found everything I expected and much much more," he went on softly. "You're a very beautiful woman, Holly."

His words made her body tingle. "You've got quite a line there, Mr. Roberts," she said, fighting to keep her voice light. *And even though I recognize it for what it is, God help me, it's still working!*

"The truth is never a line. I meant every word I said." A smile played at his mouth as he added, "And some I haven't said."

"Well then," she replied, wondering where he had learned to reduce a woman's insides to jelly in fifty words or less, "it would be better not to say them, wouldn't it?"

"Still afraid?"

"Not afraid. Cautious. I'm just not into casual affairs."

"And you think I am?"

"I hope you're not going to tell me you haven't had your share of romances."

His eyes regarded her frankly. "I won't deny that I have. But I like to think they've been mutually satisfying. I've taken, but I've given of myself as well."

Holly looked down at her plate. She didn't want to think of the times Kirk had given himself to other women. More important, she didn't want to admit that she cared.

His gaze skimmed her face and dress then returned meaningfully to her eyes. "Is there anyone special in your life?"

Holly looked up, startled. "You mean a boyfriend? No."

"Have you ever been married?"

"No, but—"

"Then the only one you really have to worry about is yourself. Right?"

"Yes, but what does that have to do with . . . with what we were talking about?"

"You mean making love?" His eyes twinkled with a mischievous light. "Nothing. Except that it's good to know there are no complications."

"You mean like old husbands or boyfriends waiting to spring out of a closet?"

He grinned. "Something like that." He turned her hand over, running his fingers gently across the upraised palm. "Did you mean what you said about never having an affair with someone from the rig?"

Holly nodded, trying to ignore the fire which had ignited beneath his touch. "I decided . . . I decided from the beginning that it wouldn't be smart. My position's too vulnerable."

He studied her face, wondering whether to believe her. "That's a pretty high price to pay for your job, don't you think?" He kept his eyes teasing, his voice light. "Haven't you ever been tempted? Just a little?"

"All right," she admitted, smiling despite herself. "The thought's crossed my mind once or twice. But not for long." Until now, she added silently.

He continued to search her face, trying to sift through the layers of her defenses. He could find no lie. Shaking his head at last, he gave her hand a final squeeze and reached for the check. "I guess we'll just have to see that the thought sticks around a little longer, won't we?"

Holly's apartment was only a short distance from the restaurant. But then none of Morro Bay was very far from the Embarcadero. Six months ago she'd rented a modest, one bedroom apartment several blocks up from the aquarium. The rooms were large and the kitchen recently remodeled. What had really sold her on the apartment, however, was its unobstructed view of Morro Rock and the bay from both the living room and bedroom windows. Holly never tired of waking up to the sight of the ocean first thing in the morning, and looking out at the moonlit harbor before going to bed at night.

"I usually walk," she told Kirk as they got back into his Corvette for the short ride. "Or ride my bike. That's one of the nice things about Morro Bay. Everything's handy."

"Is it always this quiet?" There was almost no one out-of-doors, although the evening was mild and for once, relatively free of wind. A few customers walked languorously out of neighboring restaurants, but other than that they passed only a handful of people during their drive up the hill. "While we were in there eating I think the street rolled up and tucked itself into bed for the night."

"It's pretty quiet during the week. This weekend the town will come alive, especially during the day. That's when the tourists descend."

"You sound like a native."

"I come from a small town like this, only not on the ocean. Of course Gilroy doesn't get many tourists,

69

except once a year at the Garlic Festival. But I think most small towns are basically the same."

"Small town girl leaves home to become famous oil company engineer." His smile was a vague impression in the dim glow of the street lights.

"Not quite. But I'm working on it." They were almost at her apartment, and for the first time since they'd left the restaurant, Holly was uncomfortable. "Well," she said rather inanely as he pulled the car to a stop and turned off the engine. "We're here."

"I thought of going somewhere else but—"

"Everything else is asleep," she finished for him. And I'm as nervous as a fifteen-year-old on her first date, she thought. Just make sure he doesn't come up, Holly, the little voice cautioned. Under no circumstances is he to go up those stairs!

"I don't suppose you'd like to come up for a cup of coffee?" she said over the warning screech of her better judgement. Of course he wants to come up, you idiot! Why else is he sitting there grinning like a cat who's cornered a canary?

"I thought you'd never ask," he answered, and the grin deepened to something that sent chills down Holly's spine.

"Just for coffee," she added as he came around and helped her out of the car. "No funny business."

His face was a mask of innocence as they walked up the stairs to her second-floor apartment. "Do I look like a man who would engage in funny business?" he asked.

"Unfortunately, yes." Holly slipped the key into the lock, thankful she'd taken time to do up her laundry and the dishes before setting out for the aquarium that morning.

The living room was spacious, the nicest room in the three-room apartment. Two doors, one on either side of the room, led off into the bedroom and the kitchen.

In the center of the living room, cantilevered out over the apartment below, were three large picture windows overlooking Morro Bay. At night it was too dark to see much more than the frothy outlines of waves as they beat into the inlet, but Morro Rock was outlined clearly against the glow of the three-quarter moon.

Holly was proud of the view, and of her apartment. It was a friendly home, furnished in treasured odds and ends brought with her from home, and newer items accumulated over the five years she'd been on her own. Over the sofa hung an original seascape painted by an artist friend from college. Two straight-backed antique chairs and several throw cushions bore the evidence of her mother's needlepoint efforts. A long credenza stationed against a wall featured a collection of Mexican pottery and a unique assortment of seashells she'd gathered on her travels up and down the California coast.

The wall between the bay windows and the kitchen door was hung with photographs: her mother and father at their wedding, Holly at various swim meets holding an impressive array of ribbons and trophies, her older brother, Bill, as a freckled-face youth and at his college graduation three years before her own. And finally, more recent pictures of her parents standing with their grown children in front of the family's comfortable Gilroy home.

Holly turned off the overhead light and switched on a lamp next to an overstuffed chair by the window.

"Make yourself at home," she said, heading for the kitchen. "It'll only take a minute to get the pot going." To her dismay, he followed her into the kitchen.

With fingers which seemed suddenly to have become all thumbs, Holly rinsed out the coffeepot and filled it with cold water. She was scooping in carefully measured portions of ground coffee when he came to stand beside her.

"Is that your brother in the pictures?" he asked, reaching into a cupboard for a couple of stoneware mugs. "The guy with all the freckles?"

Holly nodded as she turned on the electric burner and put on the coffee pot. "Bill's a great brother. In fact, he's a great everything. He teaches civics and English composition at Gilroy High. When Dad retired last year, Bill took over coaching the school's football and baseball team, too. He's married with three kids. A very devoted family man."

"The all-American small town family," Kirk said, finding sugar and two spoons to go along with the cups.

Something in the way he spoke made Holly look at him curiously, but she could read nothing in his face. He was lifting the pages of the hand-painted calender which hung on the wall next to the stove—made by the same artsy friend from college—so it was hard to tell. But there was something there. What? A kind of envy?

"I don't know if I'd put it like that, but I guess we were pretty normal. We're still close. I go home every month or so for a visit."

He let down the calender and removed a handful of chocolate chip cookies from a crockery jar on the counter. "My favorite kind," he explained with a grin. "Why Holly?"

"You mean my name? I popped in on my parents two days before Christmas."

"What a nice present that must have been," he said, and his expression made her feel it was true. Holly flushed.

"What about your family?" she asked him, anxious to change the subject.

"Nothing unusual," he answered, rearranging the daisy-shape magnets on her refrigerator door. "One mother, one father, one fairly standard childhood."

She waited for a moment, but when he added nothing more to this sparse biography, she asked, "But where did you grow up? Where's your home?"

"San Francisco." He nodded to the pot on the stove. "Coffee's done."

Holly's next question was quickly forgotten at the sight of the overflowing pot. Grabbing a kitchen mitt, she pulled the coffee off the stove and onto a pad next to the sink.

"I forgot to turn the burner down," she said, embarrassed.

"No problem. It smells great."

Kirk brought over the two mugs and filled them with steaming coffee while Holly arranged a tray with the sugar and cookies. When the cups were ready, he carried the tray into the living room and set it down on an end table by the couch. While she nibbled absently at a cookie and sipped her coffee, he asked more questions about her life in Gilroy, California, about her parents and about her brother. He wanted to know what her family thought about her being an oil engineer.

"Mom thinks it's great. I suspect Dad's always wondered why any woman would choose to work on an oil rig, but he's much too sweet to say anything. In fact, they probably would have gone along with my choice if I'd decided to be a ditch digger. They're like that . . . very supportive."

"And your brother?"

"Oh, Dad couldn't be happier that Bill went into education," she answered, realizing she was babbling like a brook and also that she was totally helpless to stop. "But then I don't think there was ever much doubt what Bill would do with his life. He was always great with younger kids. I used to get angry because he got more baby-sitting jobs then I did. During vacation and after school, Bill used to help Dad coach."

Kirk was sitting back on the couch watching her. "It must be nice knowing what you want out of life." He was holding the mug between his hands, his fingers curving around it, almost caressing its warmth. She watched him lower his head and take a deep sip. "I'd like to meet your brother."

"You'd like him." To her dismay, Holly kept imagining those long fingers holding onto her the way they were grasping the cup. She remembered the way they'd felt this afternoon when he'd taken her into his arms on the beach. She forced her eyes back to his face. Be calm, Holly. Be calm, think clearly and for God's sake keep your distance! "Everyone likes Bill," she went on. "He's that kind of person."

"You're that kind of person, too," he said softly.

"That's the Bishop family all right, very easy to like," she said gaily, then felt silly. How could a few innocuous words throw her into such utter confusion? It was time for a strategic retreat.

Nervously, she stood, spilling what was left of her cookie onto the rug. "Your cup's empty. I'll bring in the pot."

Kirk reached out and took her arm. "No, don't run off. I can drink coffee anytime. Right now I want to talk."

Reluctantly, Holly settled back onto the couch. But because Kirk's hand had guided her down, she was sitting much closer to him now. Too close.

She cleared her throat. "All right. What do you want to talk about?"

"Us."

"Us? There is no 'us.'" Holly felt the sudden acceleration of her heart. "And there's not going to be any us." She eyed him warily. "You promised no funny business."

"I'm not laughing, honey. Believe me, out of all the emotions I'm feeling right now, not one of them could be labeled humorous."

Holly wasn't laughing either. Kirk's eyes had become deep, expressive pools revealing his thoughts much too clearly. His desire fed her own and she felt weak.

"We've gone through all this," she said softly.

"You've gone through it. I've listened." His fingers moved down her arm to rest on the hands that were clasped tightly in her lap. "Holly, you're so tense from fighting this that you look like you're about to snap in two. Let go. Listen to what your body's trying to tell you."

Not while my mind's screaming danger with every move you make, Kirk Roberts! She tried to slide away from him but he had anticipated the move and she felt his other hand on her waist. His touch was so palpably electric that she paused, unsure, not wanting to move, petrified to stay.

He shifted on the couch until she was cradled in his arms. His lips brushed along the line of her neck, his soft breath as soothing and intoxicating as the finest liqueur. "Relax. It's all right. It's good."

And it was good. It was as if she belonged there in his embrace. The hand around her shoulder was moving lazily up and down her arm, a slow, hypnotic motion which soothed and relaxed, made no demands. After a few minutes, Holly felt her muscles unwinding. And as they loosened, she became conscious of a new feeling, a tingling sensation that seemed to be filling her body with tiny bubbles. His face tilted to rest lightly against her head, and the bubbles expanded, threatening to explode. She closed her eyes. It was good. With a long sigh, she finally let go of the tightness in her neck and arms, settling against him and opening herself to this strange, yet wonderful experience. It was very good.

"That's better," he said, his voice smoky and deep, adding to her awareness of him. "Much, much better."

Without thinking, Holly let her fingers run over the hand which rested so gently on her arm, feeling the calluses which told of years of work beneath the sea, feeling the warmth and strength there, too. Through a mist of growing desire, she moved his hand slightly until it brushed against the side of her breast. He left it there, massaging softly, his touch light. Her answering sigh was involuntary.

"Touch me. Please touch me, Kirk," she whispered.

Very lightly he massaged her rib cage, almost but not quite touching her breasts. The sensations he was arousing were exquisite. Holly felt herself growing lightheaded from the gentle teasing. When she could stand the sweet agony no longer she cried, "Please!"

His hands traveled up then, the work-roughened thumbs tracing tantalizing circles around her throbbing flesh. Desire was coursing through her. Holly trembled and knew immediately from the heightened pressure of Kirk's hands that he'd felt it, too.

"Do you still insist there's no 'us'?" he asked huskily, his lips brushing the silken threads of her hair. "How can you react like this and deny your feelings?"

Holly's response was muffled as his mouth closed on hers, soft and undemanding, calculated to tease and inflame. She felt herself melting beneath this subtle attack, and she tried to remember the reasons he shouldn't be here, the danger that lurked beneath Kirk's velvet touch.

But she was too distracted to remember. All the danger signals faded as his tongue probed her mouth, exploring its depths with an intimacy no other man had ever dared. Her skin tingled, sensitive to his every touch. Without an awareness of what she was doing, her arms crept around his neck, her fingers splaying through the thick folds of his hair, loving the feel, the smell, the texture of it.

She heard him groan as her fingers moved to massage his shoulders and neck, then a tremor ran through her body as his hands slid over the gossamer material of her dress to the slender indentation of her waist, and lower, to the gentle curve of her hips. When he molded her body to his, she moaned her own soft murmur of assent.

"You feel so wonderful," he whispered against her lips. "Like you belong here in my arms."

Holly tried to answer but her throat had suddenly gone too dry for speech. Then the words died on her lips as Kirk's hands skillfully lowered the back zipper of her dress and eased down the spaghetti-thin straps until he could surround the generous swell of one breast with his hand.

She gasped as her flesh touched his, but that, too, was muffled as his lips once again claimed hers with an urgency which was more of an invasion than a kiss. Eagerly her mouth yielded to the pressure and Holly felt waves of pleasure washing over her until she thought she would surely drown.

A soft, cooing noise came from deep in her chest as his thumb traced feather light circles around her naked nipples. She felt them quiver and grow hard, and she heard Kirk's throaty groan of satisfaction as his hand moved lower to massage the smooth, flat plane of her stomach.

He followed the soft lines of her body with his eyes, drinking her in like a rich, smooth brandy. She intoxicated his senses and he felt a need of her which surprised him. "I've spent all evening thinking about doing this," he murmured huskily. He knew his control was slipping. "I want to feel all of you. I want you to feel me."

His blatant words made her gasp, but whether from fear or anticipation, she couldn't be sure. Clearly Kirk took it for acquiescence, for his hands moved quickly to push her dress down over her hips. This was going too fast, much too fast.

But the alarm echoed harmlessly in her ears. It was too late for warning. She had long since passed the point of no return. On this flight, Holly knew there could be no turning back.

His mouth was branding her neck and throat with little kisses, making her sensitive skin prickle with longing. He brushed her dress onto the floor, then moved back, his breath coming in uneven gasps, his eyes drinking her in hungrily.

"You're so beautiful, Holly," he whispered. "You're doing crazy things to my insides."

With practiced skill, he eased her into a reclining position on the sofa so that he could raise her hips and pull off her hose and panties. When she lay naked beneath him, Holly felt she had never wanted a man so much. There was no stopping now, no more time to consider the consequences. The desire she felt for this man made no allowance for rational thought.

Even as he picked her up she was already fumbling at the buttons on his shirt, restless to feel his bare chest against her breasts. When he set her down gently on the bed, her eyes lingered on his body as freely and uninhibitedly as he had feasted on hers.

Stripped naked he stood before her, muscles gleaming, hair mussed where her fingers had raked through it, his eyes gleaming pools of desire. With a little sigh, she reached out her arms to him, and he quickly joined her on the bed, the hard angles of his body conforming perfectly to her smooth planes.

Kirk sucked in his breath at the promise in her eyes. He took her mouth in a deep, probing kiss while his hands roamed freely over her body, enjoying the smoothness of her, cupping and caressing each breast. Her uninhibited response fired his own need and he groaned from the sheer want of her.

His hands stroked down her hips to the gentle swell of her buttocks. He pulled her closer to him, letting her feel his desire, sensing the heightened excitement in her body as he softly teased apart her legs. Tenderly he explored the sweet, feminine regions of her body and found her ready. He sensed her growing need for him even before she whispered, "Kirk . . . please. I want you."

"Oh, darling," he moaned. "No more than I want you."

The knock on the door was loud and insistent. They

froze on the bed, their passion for each other held in terrible abeyance by the jarring intrusion.

The knock was repeated, and Kirk felt her move beneath him. He held her still. "Shhh. Maybe they'll go away."

But the next knock was accompanied by a loud voice that shattered this hope. "Open up, Holly. I know you're in there. Open the door."

They said the name together. "Sid Hohlman!"

"What the hell's he doing here?" Kirk asked, his breath still ragged with desire.

"I don't know. He's never come here before." She moved beneath him. "Kirk, I've got to answer the door."

"Why?" he said tersely. "That man's a first-class—" The rest of his words were lost in a low expletive as Kirk reluctantly shifted his weight so that she could get up. "Honey, get rid of him."

"I'll try."

Holly slipped quickly into her bathrobe and belted it tightly around her waist. The pounding on the door had grown even louder by the time she reached the living room. Gathering her wits as best she could, she opened the door.

"Mr. Hohlman, what a surprise. What are you doing here at this time of night?"

"It's about time," he said ungraciously. "You can't sleep that soundly. Besides, I saw the light on." He tried to look beyond her into the living room, but Holly stood in the way, blocking his view.

"I forgot to turn it off when I went to bed." Which was true enough. When she and Kirk had left the couch a little while ago, turning off the light was the last thing on her mind!

"Is there something I can do for you Mr. Hohlman? Are there problems on the rig?"

Hohlman craned his neck trying to see around her. "Aren't you going to ask me in?"

Holly didn't budge. "I'd like to, but it really is late. And I *was* in bed . . ." She let her words trail off meaningfully.

He didn't take the hint. "I got the impression someone was in there with you. Are you alone?"

"Who would be here at this time of night?" she said lightly, trying her best to avoid a direct lie. The urge to slam the door in the man's face was very strong. "You still haven't told me why you're here, Mr. Hohlman."

"I was driving by and saw your light on. I thought we could, uh . . . I thought this might be a good opportunity to discuss that little matter I mentioned aboard the rig the other day."

"Tonight? But it's so late." She narrowed the opening in the door slightly. "I really am tired, Mr. Hohlman. Why don't we talk about it some other time? Maybe I could meet you for lunch."

He seemed distracted by the generous display of thigh beneath her short robe. "But it's much more quiet here, my dear. If you'll just let me in I'm sure we could—"

"I never discuss business at home, Mr. Hohlman. *Anybody's* home." She closed the door another inch or two, feigned a yawn and said, "If you don't mind I'd really like to get back to bed now."

Sid Hohlman looked at her suspiciously. "Are you sure there's no one there?"

"*I'm* here. And I'm very tired. Why don't you give me a call in the morning?" Before he could object, she went on firmly, "Goodnight, Mr. Hohlman." She closed the door on his muttered objections, soundly turned the lock then leaned back against it, as if not trusting the door to stay shut.

She heard a few unpleasant words, then the sound of his footsteps going loudly down the stairs—she'd hear about that from the neighbors in the morning. But even when it was quiet she didn't move from the door, paralyzed by a fear that hadn't been there ten minutes ago. It was all happening too quickly and Holly felt exposed and vulnerable, not only because of Sid Hohlman's surprise appearance, but because a man she hardly knew was waiting in her bed.

Suddenly she was very conscious of the fact that she'd just met Kirk three days ago, that for all his arguments he was still a fellow crew member, and that he'd be gone, out of her life, in a few brief weeks. So what was he doing in her bed? What was she doing stark naked beneath this terrycloth robe?

She gave a silent groan. Now what, Holly Bishop, she asked herself shakily. What happens when the party's over, only the guest of honor doesn't know it yet?

Hesitantly, she turned back to the bedroom, her footsteps slowly measured, prolonging the inevitable. He was sitting up in bed watching her, hands folded behind his head, seemingly relaxed despite the fact that he wasn't wearing a stitch of clothing. It struck Holly as incongruous that, under the circumstances, she should be the one to feel embarrassed.

"Persistent isn't he?"

Holly nodded stiffly. "He doesn't like to take no for an answer."

"Neither do I."

Kirk was regarding her with an impassive look. She tried, but couldn't read his expression. It might be anything from frustration to regret, but at least he didn't seem outright furious with her.

"It's late," she said awkwardly, thinking she was beginning to sound like a broken record. "I'd . . . I'd like to go to bed now."

"I thought we had. Only not quite with the results I'd had in mind." His voice was low, but not ungentle. Despite his disappointment, and yes, hurt, Kirk hadn't gotten where he was in his profession without learning patience. He knew when to retrench. He also knew when to come back to try another day.

He got up from the bed and started to dress. Holly watched him nervously, not understanding the new feeling which had taken over now that the fear had receded. Why was he taking it so well? Why wasn't he ranting or raving or something?

"It's . . . it's just as well we were interrupted," she told him, then realized the statement had come out sounding more like a question. Who was she trying to convince, she wondered, Kirk or herself?

"Is it?" His eyes mocked hers and she knew he sensed her confusion.

Holly made an effort to take charge of the situation. "Of course. It stopped us from making a mistake we both would have regretted tomorrow."

He had finished zipping up his pants and was gazing at her with a glimmer of the desire that had burned in his eyes before. She tried to ignore the fresh warmth it sent through her body. But when he walked over and took her into his arms, there was no denying the quickened beat of her pulse.

"Honey, there is no way I am going to regret making love to you. And it is going to happen. I promise. When the time's right it'll be very special— for both of us. That's a promise, too."

He kissed her forehead lightly, inhaling the clean, sweet smell of her skin and hair. Then the tremors of longing came again and threatened his control and he broke away.

"'Nite," he said lightly, fighting the urge to reach out for the softness which had so nearly been his. "Sleep tight. I'll see you tomorrow." And he walked through the living room and was gone.

Holly went to the window and watched him enter the Corvette and pull out into the darkened street. She stood there for a long time after the sleek white bullet of a car had passed out of her vision, her head resting heavily against the sill.

When Holly finally went back to bed that night, she did not sleep tight at all.

5

The Morro Bay Weekly arrived every Friday just before noon. This Friday it was early, and Holly found it tucked into her mailbox when she left for the aquarium the next morning. She also found her picture, blown up to quarter-page size, staring out at her from the front page. Next to her was Sid Hohlman. They were both lying on the deck of Platform Kathy, buried beneath several slimy inches of drilling mud.

"Oh, no," she moaned, quickly stuffing the paper under her arm.

Looking around furtively, she hurried down the street. Two blocks later it occurred to her that hiding the paper under her arm would keep the story from only one Morro Bay resident, herself. Feeling foolish, she sat down on the nearest bus stop bench, tugged the paper out from under her arm and braced herself for the worst.

She wasn't disappointed. In his own, inimitable style, Mike Rafferty had managed to convey the message that if Worldwide Oil couldn't be counted on not to drown its own employees, how could it be trusted to follow more serious safety procedures concerning oil spills and blowouts? Great! For the past year the company had been staging an uphill battle to gain Morro Bay's trust. Now, in one, inept flick of the wrist, she had undermined all their efforts. So much for community relations!

Holly folded up the paper and continued her walk toward the aquarium, her step slower now. She would hear from Sid Hohlman, she thought grimly. As sure as Minxie loved fish, she knew this story would not go down well with Worldwide's regional manager.

"Your boss isn't going to like this," Josie said when she reached the aquarium.

"No kidding," Holly answered dryly.

"So what are you going to do?"

"I haven't the foggiest. Set sail for Tahiti? Look for a deserted cave on the Siberian coast?" Behind the gift shop the seals were barking for their morning allotment of fish. Holly wished life could be that simple for homo sapiens.

Josie was shaking her head. "You couldn't really lose your job over this, could you?"

"I don't think so. Besides, Hohlman doesn't have that kind of authority. He'd have to bring it up before the corporate brass. But he can make life even more uncomfortable for me. If that's possible."

"He's still on that track?"

Holly nodded. "Last night he came to my apartment."

Josie reached for a cigarette. "No kidding. What did

he want?" Her long fingers snapped the lighter as she muttered. "As if I didn't know."

"He wanted to talk to me about my attitude. He says I'm not being cooperative."

Josie stared at her wide eyed. "Unbelievable! That man's got more nerve than my second husband, Sam. I hope you sent him packing."

"I closed the door in his face." She hesitated. "Josie, Kirk was there."

"There? You mean in your apartment?"

Holly nodded.

"And Sid Hohlman interrupted you."

Holly smiled wanly. "Are you sure you weren't hiding in a closet?"

"I don't need to stoop to that. It's all there on your face." She took a thoughtful drag of her cigarette. "Good grief. That man is a jerk, isn't he? And I don't mean Kirk Roberts."

"Maybe it was just as well. That man is trouble, Josie. And I do mean Kirk Roberts."

"I should be blessed with such trouble." Josie regarded her friend over the counter. "Don't tell me, I can figure the rest out all by myself. After Hohlman left you told Kirk to leave."

"What else could I do?"

"Oh, honey, if you have to ask that question you *are* in trouble."

"Josie, I don't want that kind of relationship. It's asking for misery I just don't need."

"If you're so damn sure about what you need, why do I detect a suspicious moisture in your eyes?"

"With that man I can't be sure of anything. In three days he's turned my life inside out. When I'm with him I feel . . ." Holly struggled for the right words. "Good

87

lord, Josie, I'm twenty-seven years old. Yet Kirk Roberts has brought out feelings in me I didn't know existed."

"And you're complaining?"

"I'm trying to understand. I don't like being buffeted around like this. I feel out of control."

"So with a guy like Kirk Roberts who wants control?" Josie crushed out her cigarette and stepped around the counter to put a slim arm around Holly's shoulders. "Honey, take it from someone who's been there more times then she'd care to remember. Men have been using women since Adam left Eve holding the apple in the garden. But times have changed. Nowadays a relationship doesn't have to end in 'till death do us part.' Sometimes, 'it's been great fun' leaves a hell of a lot less scars. If you like the guy, enjoy him. When it's over, cut your losses and walk away."

"I don't know, Josie. I'm not sure I can do that."

"Don't knock it until you've tried it." Josie grinned and gave Holly's shoulders a final squeeze. "Think about it, hon. Believe me, when it comes to men, I know of what I speak."

Holly spent the rest of the morning thinking about it, and by noon was no closer to a solution than when she'd started. Every time she found herself envying Josie's freewheeling views on love and sex she remembered the time when, after too many gin and tonics, her friend had confided how shattered she'd been by the failure of her three marriages. Maybe it was easier to talk a good battle than to actually fight it, Holly decided. Even the most logical arguments seemed to crumble when the heart got involved.

At twelve thirty, Holly took lunch orders and walked

around the block for sandwiches. When she returned Josie was waiting with a message.

"Kirk called," she said. "Something unexpected must have come up on the platform. He said to tell you he had to go back out there with the supply ship." She was watching her friend's face closely. "He sounded real sorry to go."

Holly smiled, said fine, then found she had no appetite for the corned beef on rye with extra mustard and dill pickles she'd bought. Later, when she found herself giving the puffer fish their second meal in half an hour she admitted the truth. She was disappointed. The fact that she was angry at herself for being disappointed was too confusing to pursue, and after another hour of perfunctory dabbling around the aquarium, she left for the day.

Too restless to return directly to her apartment, Holly wandered down the Embarcadero. At the foot of the boulevard, she climbed the steps to the top of the Centennial stairway and sank onto one of the wooden benches.

In front of her loomed Morro Rock, the ancient volcanic monolith making a formidable sentry just outside the city. To either side were the seafood restaurants and curio shops so popular with the tourists. Directly below lay Morro Bay's giant walk-on chessboard. This afternoon the twenty-pound chess pieces stood silent and still; most people had finished lunch and were either back at work or roaming the shops.

She watched the sun begin its daily trek into the western sky, while flocks of seagulls soared and swooped in their endless search for fish. It was quiet, just the way Holly most enjoyed the town. The afternoon breeze coming in over the harbor felt cool and salty on her face. She supposed this serenity was one of Morro Bay's major attractions. It provided an escape from the hectic pace of city life and a chance to slip back into a simpler time. For a short while it was possible to forget that another kind of life existed beyond the borders of the quiet bay. She wished it was enough to make her forget Kirk Roberts.

Holly leaned her head back on the redwood bench and let the sights and sounds and smells of the harbor swirl over and around her and fill her with their own special peace. Kirk was twenty miles away by now and the rig was the barest dot on the horizon. Just as well, she told herself. Business and pleasure do not mix.

But when the man responsible for that pleasure was Kirk Roberts, when he was tall and blond and gorgeous and could melt a woman's heart with one smile—well, that sensible bit of philosophy became just a little harder to swallow.

Carl Morris sat across from Holly in the crew's dining room, a freshly filled cup of coffee in his hand. In front of him, a few red and white scraps were all that remained of a large dish of fresh strawberry shortcake. The toolpusher looked content.

"What happened between you and Sid Hohlman last week?" he asked, sticking a toothpick in the side of his mouth. "That guy was asking more questions about you the other day then the IRS."

Holly looked up from her own dessert. "What kind of questions?"

"Oh, like who are you dating now? And have I ever known you to, ah, entertain a male crew member in your apartment?"

Holly nearly choked on a strawberry. "He asked you *that?*"

"And more, which propriety prohibits me from mentioning." He sipped his coffee. "Would you care to enlighten the old prince here about what is going on?"

"Carl I just can't believe he'd pry like that. What business is it of his who I date?"

"Absolutely none. A fact I didn't hesitate to point out." Gingerly, he moved the toothpick to the other side of his mouth. "You could report him to the company office."

"I know." Holly thought of the picture on the front page of the *Weekly*. "But I'd just as soon keep a low profile right now."

"Can't say that I blame you," he said, accurately guessing her thoughts. "It was a dandy picture, though. Too bad Rafferty had to ruin it with that story."

"He's afraid of change, Carl." She scooped up the last of her shortcake. "So are a lot of other people in town. It's up to us to show them we don't want to see their harbor destroyed any more than they do."

"That's quite an order. Every time I walk through Morro Bay I feel about as welcome as a coyote in a chicken coop. How do you manage it?"

"I've learned to ignore some of the more blatant snubs. And I've made some good friends. Especially at the aquarium."

"If anything's going to help our image it's the work you're doing with all those fish." Carl rose and stacked his dishes onto the tray. "Worldwide ought to give you a bonus for services above and beyond the call of duty." He waited for her by the door. "Going to the movie tonight?"

"I don't think so. I'm pretty tired. Think I'll turn in early." She paused outside to button up her jacket against the brisk wind. "Enjoy the show."

"Don't worry, I will." He gave her a wink. "Raquel Welch is in it."

As Holly walked to her cabin, she thought again about Sid Hohlman. It made her burn to think he'd sneak behind her back like that to ask questions that were patently none of his business. What was he up to? she wondered uneasily. What could he hope to gain by prying into her personal life? Kirk was right, it would take more than that kind of indiscretion to get her fired. So what was he after? Even more to the point, what could she do about it?

Holly was still mulling this over when she passed the deck decompression chamber. Inside, she knew that Kirk and Don Cassill were midway through a twelve-hour decompression stint, the result of another preliminary "bounce" dive that afternoon. The knowledge that he was so close, yet for all practical purposes so far away, made her spirits plummet even further.

Holly hadn't seen him once since she'd returned to the platform that morning, at least not to speak to. She'd caught sight of him early in the afternoon while he was preparing for the dive, but he hadn't seen her. Well, she hadn't exactly sought him out. Instead she had vacillated all morning, hoping she'd bump into him and hid behind some piece of equipment whenever a tall blond head came in sight. No one had ever told her sitting on the fence could be so exhausting. If she continued like this all week she'd be a wreck by her next "seven-off."

Holly tucked a blanket snuggly into the rim of the bunk above hers, providing the only privacy she had from her five male roommates—all of whom seemed to have joined Carl at the movie—and tried to pretend that Kirk Roberts had never come into her life. An offshore oil rig was a terrible place for a romance, she told herself. Having an affair with a crew member was sheer insanity, she added. She'd worked too hard to get where she was to louse it up now, she finished with relish.

Her last thought as she drifted into slumber was to wonder if she'd see Kirk at breakfast. Which just goes to show that some people never learn, she chided herself sleepily, and then, thankfully, thought no more.

Kirk wasn't around in the morning. In fact, she didn't see him once during the next four days. Having begun the actual repairs on the rig, Kirk and his men were making "saturation" dives now, staying pressurized for days on end while they worked below and spending all their time between dives in the deck decompression chamber. She knew the divers preferred this method because they could work long stretches of time without worrying about decompressing in-between. At the end of the job, their total decompression time would be no longer then if they'd been down for only a few hours.

The week wasn't without its share of excitement, though. On her third day on, Sid Hohlman made another of his impromptu appearances, this time ostensibly to complain about Carl Morris's daily morning report, which for some unclear reason, was not to his satisfaction. But though his business was with the toolpusher, Hohlman barely nodded to Carl before cornering Holly for coffee in the dining room. He was even more furious over the newspaper article than she'd anticipated. She owed him an apology, he fumed, an apology made in the privacy of his apartment, he'd added. When Holly calmly pointed out that she had already apologized and had no intention of going to his apartment to offer another apology, he stalked off in a huff. But as she caught sight of Sid Hohlman's florid face entering the helicopter, Holly had the sinking feeling she hadn't heard the last of the matter at all.

Fortunately, the week brought good news as well. The concensus of opinion was that they were getting close to striking oil on number five well. Holly kept careful tabs on the hole depth, and was pleased that their progress was so steady.

Perhaps the best sign of all that they were getting close was the increase in betting by the drill crew over what day they would actually hit. Always a bit conservative, Carl had chosen July 20th as the big day. Ever the optimist, Holly went with July 10th, which was less than four weeks away. When the toolpusher playfully accused her of wishful thinking, Holly told him, "Never underestimate a woman's intuition, Carl. I have a sixth sense about these things."

"You mean you've got all the data," he'd thrown back. "Don't forget I know how to read those charts, too. And I plan to start paying a lot more attention now that I've got five dollars riding on the outcome."

Holly had laughed and felt good. Several days of stewing about Sid Hohlman had convinced her there wasn't a darn thing to be gained by worrying. She would face the next scene in that little drama when, and if, it came.

She was even feeling better about Kirk. Every day it seemed a little easier to slip back into P.K.R.D., a term she'd coined to mean Pre-Kirk-Roberts-Days. In fact, the time they'd spent together in Morro Bay was fading until sometimes it seemed as if it had never happened at all. Occasionally the episode in her apartment seemed very real—usually just before she fell asleep at night—but more often than not she looked back on it as a pleasant, if improbable dream.

On the last morning of her week-on, they were laying new pipe on number five when Holly's carefully nurtured complacency slipped a notch or two. Carl and the crew had just finished swinging the kelly over the joint in the new pipe, when one of the roughnecks slipped on the wet deck and fell to the floor. In the scramble to get to his feet the man slipped again, this time hitting his head hard against the heavy breakout tongs which the crew were using to unscrew the pipes. He was knocked unconscious.

The first-aid crew were on the scene in minutes, and Holly was on her way with them to the sick bay when she saw Kirk. He was standing on the top of the next deck, face chalky white, eyes wide as they stared down at the scene by the drill. Holly's heart gave an involuntary lurch. Their eyes met for only a moment, but in that time she felt as if she'd been physically run over by a bulldozer.

His face haunted her for the rest of the day. All afternoon she found herself looking over her shoulder wondering if he would suddenly appear again. So much for "it's been great fun," she thought wearily. Obviously she wasn't ready to play in Josie's league if just the sight of the man could throw her metabolism into an uproar for an entire day.

By dinner time she was exhausted, and Holly suspected it had a lot more to do with her inner turmoil than with the fact that she had just put in a grueling week aboard the rig. She shared a table with nine other crew members, ate perfunctorily and paid almost no attention to the easy banter which inevitably made up dinner conversation.

After she bussed her dishes to the counter, Holly went to her cabin and packed her few personal possessions for the trip ashore in the morning. Then, too tense to go directly to bed, she pulled on her jacket and went up on deck for some fresh air.

Holly loved the platform at night. The rig seemed almost festive in the darkness, like a brightly decorated Christmas tree against the black void of the sea. Twenty-four hours a day, seven days a week they drilled, and the whine and rumble and clanging of engines, pumps, drills and compressors was constant. It was never silent, never idle; its crew always on call.

But Holly had come to love the smells and the noise and the excitement. For all the hard, sometimes bitter work, there were compensations, not just monetary, but on a more subtle level. There were the continual challenges to be met which sent her adrenalin pumping and her heart racing and made her feel ten feet tall when she succeeded.

And there was the camaraderie. People who probably wouldn't have bothered to say hello to each other off the rig formed special bonds out here. Crews worked, played and lived together. They depended on each other for their jobs and for their safety. There was a warm feeling of belonging and of being respected and Holly wouldn't have traded it for the world.

As usual, the walk was relaxing her. She breathed deeply of the brisk sea air and felt some of her tenseness dissipate. Then she rounded the corner just opposite the number five derrick and saw him, and in one, quick flip of the heart, Holly felt as though she were going to dissolve.

He was standing with his back to her, arms resting easily on the guardrail, looking out over the ocean. For a moment she couldn't be sure it was he, then he turned slightly and she saw his profile clearly in the light of the full moon. Every nerve ending in her body froze as she fought down the impulse to run over and throw her arms around him. Calm down, Holly, she told herself. There is nothing to get excited about. Just turn around very quietly and walk back the other way before he sees you.

But it was too late for retreat. Kirk had caught her first startled movement and was already looking in her direction. Of her two choices—stay or run—Holly decided it was far more mature to walk over, say hello and goodnight and leave. She could do that, she told herself. Any three-year-old could do that.

Holly couldn't do that. She managed the short walk over to the railing all right, but when she tried to speak she found her voice had suddenly gone too hoarse to be heard over the incessant clamor of machinery. Quickly implementing an alternate plan, she nodded silently, swallowed hard, and joined him at the rail to look quietly out at the sea.

Kirk was surprised but was afraid to speak for fear of scaring her off. Having her join him like this was uncanny. Since the accident on deck this afternoon, he'd been unable to get her out of his thoughts or to forget his initial panic when he thought that she'd been the injured crewman on the number five well. His relief to find that she wasn't—well, he was still trying to puzzle that one out. In fact, that was why he'd come out on deck tonight, to try to sort out feelings that were getting altogether too complex for his liking. But now that she was here the questions could wait until later. It was enough to have her beside him, to feel her warmth and softness next to him on the cold deck.

They stood like that for a long time, an eternity, Holly thought, before he finally spoke. "You know, it's funny," he said without turning his head away from the moonlit sea. "The decibel level out here is high enough to give an audiologist ulcers. Yet it's peaceful. Strange, isn't it?"

"I don't know," Holly answered, relieved to find her voice functioning near normal again. "I guess it depends on your definition of peaceful. Sometimes I think that anyone who works on an oil rig has got to march to a different drummer."

Kirk turned until he was facing her, his back resting comfortably against the rail, arms folded across his chest. "And what drummer does Holly Bishop march to?"

"I'm not sure," she answered honestly. "I've never thought of myself as being very different from anyone else."

"No, I guess being a lady mud engineer is pretty common." Her face shone softly in the moonlight, her eyes deep, dark pools holding a promise even she didn't realize. This time he couldn't resist the urge to run a hand gently over the curve of her cheek. "And they're all gorgeous brunettes, too," he said more quietly. "Yup, I'd say you're pretty common, all right."

Holly felt the familiar volt of electricity which seemed to emanate from his fingertips, and then the weakness which always followed it. She curled her hands tightly around the railing to keep them still; the urge to touch him in return was almost overpowering.

Keep it steady, Holly, she told herself sternly. Very, very steady.

"What about you?" she asked in defense. "Anyone who deep-sea dives for a living isn't marching along to John Philip Sousa."

He laughed. "Maybe not, although it seems perfectly natural to me. But then I guess you could say the same thing. Maybe we're both mavericks."

"Mmmm. Holly Bishop, maverick." She found the notion appealing. "I think I like it."

This time when he laughed he encircled her shoulders with his arm. "Good. We're progressing." Before she could ask him what he meant by that remark, he went on, "You're off tomorrow, aren't you?"

Holly nodded, not sure what was coming next. He'd all but ignored her for the past seven days. Why show an interest in her time off now?

"We've got supplies coming in from L.A. Until they get here we've got some time on our hands. How about dinner tomorrow night?" Catching Holly's expression he went on, "Hey, don't look so scared. I didn't say you were going to be part of the menu."

"I'm just surprised, that's all," she said, annoyed that his shot had come so close to the mark. "I thought you'd be working all next week."

"Even divers who don't march to John Philip Sousa take time off once in a while. Overwork does not increase job efficiency."

"No, I guess not." Holly said the words at normal volume and Kirk bent his head to catch what she was saying. Louder, she went on, "I don't think dinner's a good idea."

"Why not?" His gaze was much too penetrating, and Holly knew she wasn't hiding her feelings very well. "You're still thinking about last time, aren't you?"

"No, of course not, I—" She saw the raised eyebrow and realized she wasn't fooling anyone, least of all Kirk Roberts. "Oh, all right. What if I am?"

"I think we should talk about it."

"What's to talk about? We both got carried away. It was as much my fault as yours."

"Honey, what happened between us wasn't a matter of fault, it was a miracle. And not talking about it won't make it go away."

Holly ran a tongue around her dry lips. It might not take it away, but it was a whole lot easier on her nervous system. "You started the saturation dives this week," she said, changing the subject. "How do the repairs look so far?"

He took so long to answer that she thought for a moment he hadn't heard her question. "They're coming along okay. We went at it pretty hard this week."

"So I noticed." The response, and the tone, had been involuntary and Holly hoped he missed it. He didn't.

"You think I've been avoiding you?"

"Don't be ridiculous. Why should I think that?"

"Because it's true. Lady, I've been staying as far away from you as possible. Wait," he went on before she could pull away. "I had a darn good reason. Everytime I see you I want to do a whole lot more than just say, 'Hi, lady engineer, how's the mud mixture today?' And if you don't think it's frustrating seeing you out here day after day and knowing there's not one damn thing I can do about it . . ." His voice trailed off helplessly, but Holly understood. He might have been describing her own feelings. And there wasn't one damn thing she could do about it either.

She shivered, but not from the wind, which had turned into a brisk southwesterly. "I don't . . . I don't think we should have dinner together."

His arm slipped down around her waist and the other moved to tilt up her chin. "I think we should. Like I say, ignoring it isn't going to make it go away."

But it's a whole lot safer, Holly thought, fighting the familiar spread of goose bumps down her back. This can't go on, she told herself fiercely. Saying no to Kirk Roberts was like refusing a popsicle on the hottest day of the year. She simply wanted him too much. "It's late." The words were lost on the wind and in the steady whine behind them, but she knew Kirk had heard.

He kissed her cheek lightly, tasting the salty spray on her face and wanting desperately to taste more. Kirk felt her tremble slightly in his arms and knew she wanted more, too. But because it was neither the time nor the place, he knew he had to let her go. "Get to bed, Holly. We have tomorrow. We can talk about it then."

"But I don't want—"

His lips came down softly to silence her objections. And despite herself her breath quickened at the contact, and all the objections were magically forgotten. It was a brief, intoxicating flutter of a kiss, over almost before it began. But it left Holly breathless.

"You're lying to me, honey," he breathed into her ear. "Your body's bursting with want, whether you choose to accept it or not."

As if to prove his point, Kirk's lips returned to hers, touching them lightly, drawing away, then returning to claim them more forcefully. He felt the erratic jump of her pulse where his hand cupped her chin, and the surrender of her body as she pressed herself against him. Feeling the answering beat of his own heart he pushed her away, this time with finality.

"There are some things in this life you just can't hide," he told her. "And believe me, this is one of them."

6

⚬⚬⚬⚬⚬⚬⚬⚬⚬⚬

They established an unspoken moratorium which lasted throughout dinner. Both seemed to realize that opening the Pandora's box of their feelings over savory fresh cioppino, would be tantamount to having a pillow fight at the Louvre. Later would be soon enough.

Kirk had chosen a restaurant on the road leading out of Los Osos which Holly hadn't known existed. The fish was as fresh as she'd tasted it anywhere on the coast, the atmosphere rustic and quiet.

On the drive back to Morro Bay, Holly looked up at a sky that seemed to have been cut from a smooth piece of indigo velvet, with thousands of tiny, glittering stars pasted on as an inspired afterthought. To their left, the ocean pounded onto the craggy shore, the waves were sheets of foamy turbulence in the bright moonlight. It was a beautiful night and despite the

103

trepidation she'd felt all day at going out again with Kirk, she was enjoying herself.

"It's Friday," Kirk announced, as they entered Morro Bay. "The town's allowed to stay up past its bedtime tonight. How's about a nice quiet nightcap?"

Delighted to do anything to postpone the moment when he would take her back to her apartment, Holly readily agreed. "Sounds good." She looked at the tourists milling about the Embarcadero. Several of the restaurants along the street had excellent bars overlooking the ocean and Holly assumed he'd stop at one of these. She was surprised when he turned off onto Driftwood Street.

"Where are we going?" she asked him. But he had already stopped in front of an apartment building and was turning off the ignition.

"We're here, honey."

"But where's here? I thought you said you wanted a quiet nightcap."

He got out of the car and came around to the passenger side. "I do. I also want to talk. And this is the quietest spot I know." Kirk opened the door. "Come on, I'm not going to ravish you. I promise."

Suddenly Holly felt cold and clammy. "But this . . . isn't this your apartment? You didn't tell me we were coming here."

"Would you have come if I did?" At her slowly shaking head, he went on, "That's why I thought it would be better not to announce it." His voice remained light and coaxing. "Tell you what. Come up for one drink. If you still want to leave I'll take you home—with no argument."

Holly tried to read his expression in the moonlight.

"I don't like that look on your face. You look too . . . too eager."

"Honey, in order to change that expression you'd have to radically alter nature. You're a beautiful woman, and believe me, I'm a normal, healthy male. The two add up to an eager expression in any man's language."

Holly wondered about her own expression. She couldn't deny that the feelings she was experiencing right now were every bit as normal and healthy as his. Did she want him or didn't she? For God's sake, make up your mind, Holly Bishop. What's it to be?

"All right," she told him. "But just for one drink." And if that doesn't sound phony then Worldwide's middle name isn't oil.

His apartment was modern—late California plastic was the label that leapt to mind—but it lacked identity. The three rooms were well designed but had an unsettled quality about them, as if nothing permanent had been set down, either by the owners or the present tenant. Everything had been color coordinated to offend as few tastes as possible and consequently the decor failed to rise above the level of innocuous. She could see by his few personal possessions that the apartment meant no more to Kirk than a place to sleep and eat between diving stints on Kathy.

"I don't have your talent for fixing up a place," he said, reading her thoughts. "But I'm never in a town long enough to make it worth the effort."

His words reminded her again of how transient his life was. "Don't you have a place somewhere to call home?"

"I suppose San Francisco comes as close to qualifying for that dubious honor as anywhere else," he answered. He was at the kitchen sink pouring brandy into two snifters.

"But what about your family?" she persisted. "I still know next to nothing about you."

"There's not much to tell. Fairly normal parents, fairly normal upbringing. I don't want to bore you."

Holly watched him carry their drinks into the living room, doubting that anything about Kirk Roberts could be boring. Why was he so reluctant to talk about himself?

True to his promise, they sat at opposite ends of the couch, and Kirk made no move to infringe on her territory. Holly held on tightly to her drink, thankful it gave her something to do with her hands, and thinking that this was the most awkward situation she'd ever faced in her life.

The minutes dragged. Kirk stretched out his legs, then pulled them in again; Holly nervously sipped too much of her brandy, coughed and felt ridiculous. She looked at Kirk, smiled stupidly, then looked away, aware only that he was far too handsome for any woman's peace of mind. Then the strain seemed to become too much for them and they blurted out simultaneously:

"That was terrific cioppino tonight—"

"You look beautiful tonight—"

Suddenly, Holly was struck by the humor of the situation. Here they were, two grown adults, wanting each other desperately, yet so tongue-tied they couldn't even get out one simple sentence. To Kirk's surprise, she began to laugh.

He moved next to her and one by one released the

fingers which were holding her drink in a death grip. Gently, he set the drink down on the table. "Honey, you're going to crack that glass in two. I promised not to start anything unless you gave the word. Don't you trust me?"

"No . . . yes . . . I don't know," Holly replied, too confused to think straight. Certainly she didn't trust herself—not for one heartbeating, pulse-thundering moment. She wanted him so badly right now it was all she could do not to beg him to hold her and touch her and love her. There was an ache in her so painful she thought she was going to cry. And she didn't want to cry because then he'd surely know how she felt.

As if he were tuned in to her most intimate thoughts, he said, "What do you want from me, Holly? What do you want me to do?"

There it was—on the line. No more evasion or denials. Just the plain, honest-to-goodness truth. What *did* she want from him?

"I . . . kiss me, Kirk. Please, kiss me."

As soon as the words were said a kind of peace settled over her. At the same time a wonderful, soaring kind of excitement whirled through her body, as if it had been waiting there, ready to burst forth.

"Are you sure?" No doubts this time?"

"Tons of them," she told him softly. "But at the moment I can't seem to remember a single one. I just . . . I just want you to kiss me."

"Funny," he whispered, closing the few inches still left between them. "That's exactly what I had in mind, too."

Lightly he touched his mouth to hers, then suddenly, explosively, the touch was no longer tentative. With a little groan, he took her lips with a passion that left her dizzy. His hands seemed to be everywhere at once, stroking and touching, lighting fires that quickly burned out of control. Her own hands became tangled in his hair. She drew his head down harder until the kiss created a shattering need that neither of them could contain.

"This has got to be the best idea you've had all evening," he murmured into the curve of her throat.

"Whoever said engineers weren't imaginative?" she whispered back.

"Not me, lady," he said, occupying himself with the lobe of her right ear. "It could never have been me."

Then there were no more words as their mouths melded together in a symphony of whirling, wonderful sensations. His hands found the scooped neck of her cotton dress and ran gently along the graceful curve from one creamy shoulder to the other. She trembled when his fingers brushed along the top of her dress, hooking into the spaghetti-thin straps to inch the bodice down to her waist. His gaze wandered slowly over the full curves of her breasts, and where they lingered she burned from a hunger which demanded to be satisfied.

"Kirk," she moaned. "What are you doing to me?"

"Nothing yet, honey. But wait and see. Just wait and see."

She shivered from the raw promise in his husky voice, and when his head lowered to tease and taste each dark rose-tipped breast, a slow fire began to kindle in her, starting deep within her and spreading quickly through the rest of her body. Then his hands began to slide up and down the bare skin on either side of her breasts, and the treacherous warmth threatened to consume her.

Shifting slightly, Kirk lifted Holly until he could slide the dress over her hips and onto the floor. Picking it up, he tossed it onto a nearby chair. Just as methodically, he lowered her panty hose down her long, slim legs and sent them flying to the chair.

Holly was too much under his spell to move. She could only sit helplessly, feeling the heat of his gaze on her body, knowing that all that separated him now from his goal were her delicate lace panties. And then his finger slipped beneath the elastic and they, too, were sent tumbling across the room. She heard Kirk expel a long, deep sigh, and knew that his control was as fragile as her own.

For a long moment he just sat there staring at her, his sea-green eyes dark with desire as they traveled over every softly rounded inch of her slender body. She was beautiful, and he was shocked by the depth of his longing for her. Repressing the wild urge to take her then and there, he picked her up in his arms and carried her silently to the bedroom and laid her down on the cool spread. Quickly, he stripped off his own clothes and eased himself down beside her.

His weight made the bed creak, and Holly moved beneath him until she could look directly into his eyes. His look made her feel beautiful, the depth of his longing clear as he bent to nip her lower lip with his teeth. Teasing them apart, his tongue explored every hidden corner of her mouth, laying claim to it with a mastery that left her breathless. His hands roamed over her body, cupping and stroking each breast, traveling down the smooth, easy swell of her hips. Holly put her arms around his neck, tasting him and feeling him as she had never felt a man before. His hard desire pressed into her and she groaned.

Sensing her anguish, Kirk's hand slipped between her legs, and the heat became even more intense. Over her own soft moanings, she heard him whispering her name, and the sound blended with her own cries until they peaked into a crescendo which could have only one ending.

Quickly he slid between her thighs, and eagerly she awaited him, ready to give as well as to receive. Then they came together, and Holly felt as if her mind had exploded into a million wild and wonderful pieces. Time ceased to exist beyond the here and now; there was no yesterday and no tomorrow, only she and Kirk, only this magical thing they were sharing. Again and again he filled her aching void, moving with ever increasing strokes, consuming her totally until the waves of pleasure became too much to be borne.

Holly cried out as she reached the crest, as she experienced the soaring intensity of her passion, and he smiled down at her, a part of her ecstasy, one with her joy. Then he shuddered and met his own staggering summit, pulling her with him as they crested over the top.

The next few days passed too quickly. They swam and lazed on Holly's tiny beach, sailed or fished off the pier. One afternoon they even tried their hand at playing golf. When Kirk uncharitably pronounced

Holly a duffer, she promptly aimed a neat par three over a small lake hazard, while Kirk lost two of his best balls to a watery grave.

Best of all, they made love. Whenever the spirit moved them, which was delightfully frequent, they came together beneath the Pacific sun or under the blanket of stars that covered the sleepy little bay at night. It was a beautiful week, and Holly never wanted it to end. She wouldn't allow herself to think of the time when inevitably, it would be over.

Holly still spent time at the aquarium each morning, but now Kirk went with her, and she was amazed by how easily he fit in. She already knew Josie's opinion of "The Hunk," as she had secretly dubbed him. But she was surprised to see how quickly Ginny Palermo and the rest of the staff took to him. In his comfortable, teasing way, Kirk had the girl laughing at his collection of diving tales, and Ginny was soon confiding her problems about college. Holly was amazed at the way he handled the situation; he was sympathetic but objective, caring yet not really interfering.

Even the seals took an uncanny liking to him, and Holly felt a slight pang of jealousy when, on his very first visit, Kirk had Minxie eagerly eating out of his hand. But then she realized he had them all eating out of his hand. Including herself. Heaven help her, she was every bit as susceptible to Kirk Roberts's charms as the rest of them!

Yet no matter how close she felt to Kirk, she realized she still knew next to nothing about him. Every time she brought up his family, or his home, he would politely, but effectively, change the subject. His past remained a mystery, and like most mysteries, it cried out to be solved.

One morning, something happened at the aquarium which provided the first real key to the puzzle. She and Kirk had just finished settling the last of Josie's North American fish into their new tanks, when two Morro Bay fishermen arrived with a young male elephant seal they'd rescued from the waters outside the bay. His wounds suggested that like Minxie he'd been the victim of a shark attack, a common enough occurence in those waters. One particularly vicious cut just behind the right flipper caused particular concern.

"Looks to me like the pup needs stitches," one of the fishermen told Josie, while Holly and Kirk looked on. "He lost a lot of blood while we were bringin' him in."

"Doctor Fenway's in Los Angeles," Josie told them, referring to the local veterinarian who regularly looked after the aquarium's stock. "He won't be back until tomorrow."

"I don't think it should wait that long," the second fisherman said. "Can't you call someone else?"

"I'll try Doctor Meredith in Cayucos," Josie said. "He's the next closest vet."

But Doctor Meredith was also unavailable. Josie hung up the phone and turned to the others. "Can't we tape it or something? Just until tomorrow?"

"It's too deep," Kirk told her. He was bending over the seal, gently probing around the wound with his fingers. "It needs attention right now. Do you have any surgical supplies?"

"You mean tape and scissors and stuff like that?"

"And anesthetic," Kirk added to Josie's list. "And I don't suppose you have sutures and a needle?"

Josie thought and then said, "All the medical stuff is stored in the back room. Norm used to handle that sort of thing. Let's go see what we can find."

Norm was Josie's third husband, her partner in buying the aquarium six years ago. When the marriage broke up, Norman cleaned out both bank accounts, packed up their color TV and drove off in the couple's late-model Chrysler. Josie got custody of the aquarium.

In a moment the two returned with a sealed package and several bottles. Kirk set down the supplies and turned to the fishermen. "If you'd get on either side of him and hold down his head and flippers I think we can do it. Don't hurt him, but hold him as still as you can. I'll be applying a local anesthetic, but when I actually start stitching it'll smart."

Holly stared at him. Surely he wasn't going to try anything as ambitious as sewing the wound by himself? But as Kirk scrubbed his hands and lower arms at the sink, she saw he was serious. Even more astounding, he seemed to know what he was doing!

The seal looked no more than four or five months old, yet Holly could see he already weighed over two hundred pounds. As the men moved to either side of the animal and found a hand grip, she positioned herself at the pup's head and gently stroked his face while Kirk worked. The seal looked up at her with huge, frightened eyes, and Holly bent her head to murmur soft words of assurance.

Kirk thoroughly washed the wound, disinfected it, then dabbed on a generous portion of local anesthetic. Opening the sealed package, he took out the sterile needle and deftly threaded it with a length of suturing material, then began the tedious job of joining the severed skin. The pup squealed and made an effort to squirm free, but the men tightened their grip, holding him in place. Holly could see beads of perspiration on their faces from the effort. When Kirk was finished, they all breathed a collective sigh of relief.

"There, that ought to do it," he told them. "He'll be eating you out of house and home in no time, Josie."

Holly saw the seal settled comfortably in an unoccupied enclosure where he could mend in peace, then went back inside the aquarium. The fishermen had left and Josie was up front tending the gift shop. Kirk was putting away the supplies.

"That was a pretty amazing performance," she told him. "You didn't pick that up fixing oil rigs."

Kirk smiled. "You'd be surprised what you can learn three-hundred feet down."

Holly shook her head. This time she wasn't going to be put off. It was time the missing pieces came together. "Come on, Kirk. Where did you learn to operate on seals like that?"

"That was a far cry from an operation," he told her, still smiling. "All right, all right, don't get excited. I guess I do owe you some kind of explanation."

"It's about time. After you finish up here why don't we go for a walk and you can tell me all about it."

Automatically, they turned in the direction of Holly's beach. Neither of them spoke as they made their way onto the barely visible path which led to the small clearing. It wasn't until they were seated on the sand that Holly finally prompted, "Okay, let's hear about this deep, dark past of yours."

"It's not very deep or dark," he told her. "Just something I don't usually talk about."

Holly sensed his hesitation and let him take his time.

She was even tempted to tell him she didn't need to know if it was that painful to discuss. But part of her *did* want to know. It was suddenly very important that she know everything about Kirk Roberts.

Finally, with a look that told her he was through evading, he began talking, telling her of his childhood in an exclusive San Francisco neighborhood, of being the only child of highly educated parents, of attending the finest private schools, and of being lonely.

"Dad's a plastic surgeon," he said. "A very exclusive plastic surgeon. He makes an impressive living altering noses and embarrassing bulges, or lack of bulges, on people who can afford the remodeling fee. My mother has her degree in fine arts, but she hasn't used it in years. She's very involved with her clubs and their social life."

He paused, and Holly waited for him to go on, not wanting to hurry him, content to be sharing this intimate part of Kirk's life.

"It was always assumed that I would follow in Dad's footsteps," he went on at last. "And for a while, when I was very young, I actually wanted to become a surgeon. Then, gradually, my ideas changed. I saw so little of my parents, I began to resent my father's career and my mother's social obligations."

Kirk changed positions, pulling one leg beneath his body, obviously uncomfortable with the recital. "There I was, a privileged child by anyone's standards, envying my friends who did things with their families, whose dads took them fishing or to a ball game. Poor little rich kid." Restlessly, he tossed a handful of sand at a nearby rock. "Sure you want to hear more?"

"Yes," she told him softly. "I do."

115

"After a while I rebelled against everything my parents stood for. Dad catered to very wealthy patients; Mom volunteered exclusively for causes that made the society pages. I opted for reverse snobbery. It was the rebellious sixties, remember, and I made it a point to hang out with the most disreputable types I could find. The more outlandish the cause, the more wholeheartedly I'd back it. Anything to get a rise out of my folks."

"And you succeeded?"

"Admirably. So well that in my junior year of high school they sent me off to one of the most conservative boarding schools on the East coast."

Holly saw the pain on his face and her heart constricted. "Oh, Kirk. You must have hated it."

"Enough to run away every time I got a chance. The fourth or fifth time, my father had a heart attack. Or, so they told me. What kind of son would do that to his own father? they asked. Either I stayed in school and minded my p's and q's, or for the rest of my life I could carry the guilt of putting him in his grave."

Holly was shocked. "Kirk! That was a terrible burden to put on a child."

He shrugged. "It worked. I went back to boarding school, hit the books and managed to pull my average up enough to get accepted at Harvard, although I wouldn't be surprised to find out that Dad had a hand in that, too."

"Harvard?"

"For four years. After that I attended medical school. During my second year, the Vietnam War broke out."

"And you enlisted."

"Not right away." He smiled, but the humor did not

extend to his blue-green eyes. "My folks wanted me to stay and finish my studies. The scenario called for me to join my Dad's practice after I'd completed my internship."

"What happened?"

"I played tennis one day with one of my father's associates who was in Cambridge to visit his family. When the game was over—and I'd trounced him—he mentioned that I was a real chip off the old block. The way I'd played that morning reminded him of my Dad's performance a few years back at a tournament they'd both been in." His voice had taken on an edge of bitterness. "The date of that tournament was less than two weeks after my father's supposed heart attack."

Holly couldn't speak, she could only look at Kirk's angry face and feel his pain. How could parents do that to their child? Given her own loving upbringing, she found it nearly impossible to comprehend.

"The following day I left med school and joined the navy. I had a taste of deep-sea diving and I liked it. When I found out how hazardous underwater demolition duty was, I volunteered."

"Your parents must have had a fit."

"A beaut," he said, the smile coming back. "And I'm ashamed to admit I loved every ranting minute of it. I was finally on my own and doing what I wanted to do."

"And all that medical training went out the window."

"Oh, I don't know. There's a certain elephant seal pup today who might disagree with that statement."

"Have you been happy, Kirk?"

Again there was a pause before he answered. "For the most part, yes. I enjoy my work. I love the excitement and the travel—and I like to think it's important."

"It's also dangerous."

"I suppose that's part of the attraction," he answered honestly.

"And you've been at it so long—"

"You mean that at thirty-eight it's time for me to quit." Holly nodded, and he went on, "Maybe. But old habits die hard. And I'm still good at what I do. I think there are a few more dives left in me before I hang up the flippers."

"Isn't there something . . . anything else you'd like to do?" Holly knew she was pushing him, but she couldn't help herself. She had to know.

"Mmmm." A very different sort of light had come into his eyes. "As a matter of fact there is."

"I don't mean *that*. I mean with your life."

He had shifted on the sand and was lying on his side facing her. She thought the clear blue-green of his eyes rivaled the sea in intensity. And the look they were giving her now required no translation. "Right now this is the most important thing in my life," he said softly. He ran a finger lightly up her arm. "The past is over with. The present's here waiting to be enjoyed."

She trembled slightly as his hand grazed her breast and even more when he leaned over and brought his mouth to hers. The kiss was as light as a summer breeze and just as sweet, and beneath the soft pressure her lips willingly parted. Then the kiss grew deeper and Holly felt the familiar, wonderful response growing in her.

"You're right," she murmured as they sank softly back on the sand. "There's a lot to be said for the present."

Gently, he brushed the dark hair away from her cheeks. "Mmmmm. And a lot that doesn't have to be said at all."

7

Kirk went back to the rig that evening, Holly three days later. She arrived to find the number five well with three more sections of pipe, but no oil, and Kirk in the middle of another saturation dive. The first bit of news she took in stride, the second left her unaccountably depressed, a recurring feeling which wasn't getting easier to handle with practice.

She told herself that by now she should be used to the fact that their work schedules were about as compatible as oil and water. All things considered, they were lucky to have snatched what time they'd had. She knew she should be grateful. But it was difficult to be grateful while you were lonely, and it was very easy to be lonely when you were in love.

Holly no longer bothered to deny the fact that she was hopelessly, and very probably disastrously, in love with Kirk Roberts. For a long time she had tried to ignore her feelings in the rather naive hope that they might go away. Now she knew they would never go away, that she probably didn't want them to go away, and that she didn't have a whole lot of control over them at any rate.

On her fourth morning back, after training a novice roughneck how to catch cuttings from the shale shaker, Holly headed downstairs for a quick cup of coffee. Her heart did a quick leap as she entered the dining room and saw Kirk sitting with his crew at one of the tables.

After seven days without seeing him, Holly's first impulse was to run over and throw her arms around him. Her second impulse, tempered by a moment's sensible reflection, caused her to nod pleasantly at the group, and continue on to the coffee pot. She was mentally awarding herself an Emmy when she felt a movement behind her.

"You're wearing more clothes now than the last time I saw you," he told her quietly. "I have an irresistible urge to rip them all off and see you that way again."

Holly whirled around, but Kirk was nonchalantly reaching for the pot. He didn't even glance at her as he went on, "Meet me down by the primary power unit in fifteen minutes and we'll make mad passionate love."

"You're crazy," she whispered back, absentmindedly stirring unwanted cream into her cup.

"Main power unit. Fifteen minutes."

Holly watched him walk back to his table, then took a seat on the opposite side of the room. Slowly she sipped the hot coffee, made a face at the cream and tried to keep her eyes off the divers as they rose to leave a few minutes later. The few times they'd met after dark had been dangerous enough. There was no way was she going to risk a meeting in broad daylight!

Ten minutes later, Holly was standing furtively outside the doorway to the main power center feeling like a spy from one of her James Bond movies. Waiting until the coast was clear, she crept stealthily past the bank of consoles and hurried to a back room where one of the huge turbo-electric power units was housed. Kirk was already waiting, crowded into a little corner opposite the door. The noise in the room was almost deafening, and while it would effectively keep anyone from hearing them, she thought they'd be lucky to hear each other.

"We've got to stop meeting like this," he yelled with a grin.

"That's fine with me!" Holly said leaning against the wall for support. "My heart's going a mile a minute." She looked at him accusingly. "How can you look so damn calm?"

Kirk laughed. "You'd make a lousy criminal, honey. It's just as well you've got an honest occupation."

"I don't feel particularly honest at the moment. What if the engineer comes back here and sees us?"

"Then he can eat his heart out and go find his own mud mama." He gathered her into his arms. "This one's taken."

"Kirk, this is like playing Russian roulette."

He kissed her forehead. "I know. Exciting, huh?"

His boyish grin was so infectious that Holly had to laugh. After a whole week, he looked so good to her that her breath caught in her throat. "You're more than enough excitement for this woman, Kirk Roberts. Any more and I couldn't be responsible for the consequences."

"Hmmm. I like the sound of that." She trembled as his hand found her chin, tipping her face up to meet his. "I've missed you, lady. Have you ever considered taking up deep-sea diving? I hear making love at three hundred feet is a mouth-watering experience."

"Ugh! You mean I risked my reputation for that? Kirk, be serious. I—"

Kirk was suddenly very serious, but not in the way Holly expected. His lips closed on hers in a hungry kiss that let her know very graphically just how much he'd missed her. "Mmmm," he said directly into her ear. "You taste delicious—coffee and cream."

"The cream was a mistake. You had me flustered."

His hand slipped under her jacket where it cupped a breast. "Good, that's the way it should be. A guy's gotta keep his woman on her toes." He lowered his head and nuzzled the curve of her neck. Instinctively, she raised her face to meet his, and their lips met again. His hand crept under her sweater to pull up her bra so that he could feel her aching flesh in his hands. Holly shuddered from the dual invasion.

"I dare you to tell me this isn't better than playing with mud," Kirk challenged. His hand continued its maddening journey beneath her clothes. "Honey, you've got better curves than a roller coaster. And they're a hell of a lot more exciting."

Then he was savoring her mouth again, invading it with his tongue, caressing it with his teeth, one moment harsh, the next gentle. His hand traced lazy circles around a nipple, and Holly could feel it straining and growing taut.

"Kirk," she gasped, fighting for breath. "Not here. It's too—"

Luckily, they caught sight of the engineer before he saw them. They would never have heard his footsteps over the hammering engine. By the time he came up to them they were standing a respectable distance apart, flushed and slightly disheveled, but calmly discussing the power unit's commendable performance record.

The engineer looked at them in surprise, his nerves still jangling from the shock of discovering two unexpected people in his engine room. Nodding socially, but with obvious curiosity, he went about taking his readings. When he was through, he shook his head and walked back to the control room.

Kirk and Holly were still laughing when they got back on deck.

"Did you see the look on poor Joe's face?" Holly said. "He'll be wondering about that visit all week."

"Just think of the spice we added to his job. From now on he'll never be sure what he's going to find when he comes through that door."

"Will I see you tonight?" she asked. A roustabout passed them and Holly tried to keep her face impersonal. She was not feeling impersonal.

"We start another saturation dive at five thirty tomorrow morning," he told her. "Tonight we'll be checking the equipment." His hand closed on hers where it rested on the railing. "I'm sorry, honey."

Of course. Understandable. I won't see him for at least another five days. Don't act like an idiot now, Holly. Make an effort to behave like the mature, sensible adult you're supposed to be. Her smile was bright enough to win her second Emmy award for the day. "That's okay. I understand. Work has to come first."

The devilish grin was back. "Not always."

"Often enough." The smile was making her cheeks

ache. "It's about time the world learned to do with less oil."

"Them's fightin' words, lady. Remind me to larn you some proper respect."

"Is that a threat or a promise?"

Without caring who might see them, Kirk leaned over and kissed Holly lightly on the mouth. "Honey, that's a promise you can count on!"

That afternoon when a powerboat pulled up to the platform, Holly nearly fell over the railing at the sight of Ginny Palermo at the wheel. A hundred feet above the water's surface, Holly was unable to communicate except with a broad grin. She motioned for a crewman to lower the "elevator" from the giant crane, then did an exaggerated pantomime for the girl to put on her life vest and climb aboard. Ginny looked doubtfully at the roped platform used to raise and lower crewmen from the supply ship, then, with little choice—and half a dozen people yelling encouragement to her from above—she finally climbed aboard and hung on for dear life.

"Ginny, what in the world are you doing here?" Holly asked as soon as the girl dropped onto the deck. She stopped when she saw Ginny's pale face. "No, wait. It's too noisy out here. Let's get some lunch." Firmly, Holly placed a hard hat on her friend's head. "Come on."

They sat down in a relatively unpopulated corner of the room, Holly with a steaming cup of coffee and a salad, Ginny with a large coke, french fries and a hamburger that looked big enough to feed half the crew. "Okay," Holly said as soon as they were settled. "What's going on?"

To her surprise, Ginny burst into tears. "I've . . . I've run away from home."

"You've what!" Holly was torn between the urge to wipe the girl's tears and give her a good shake. Her natural compassion won. Fishing in her jacket pocket she came up with a clean tissue. "Here, use this."

Holly waited while the girl more or less regained her composure. "More trouble with your parents?"

Ginny nodded, then gave her nose a good blow. When she had saturated that tissue, Holly handed her another. "I hope this isn't a three-tissue cry," she told her, "because that's my last one. Now will you please tell me what happened?"

Haltingly, and with enough tears to require the use of several napkins, Ginny told the story. The deadline to register for Fall semester was in less than a week, and Ginny's parents had flatly refused to allow her to attend Santa Barbara University, much less discuss her plans to major in petroleum engineering. Matters had come to a head the night before.

"I was so darn frustrated that all I could think of doing was to leave," the girl told her. "So I did."

"And came here in your father's boat."

She nodded.

"Without telling them where you were going?"

"I didn't know where I was going until I realized I had no car, and not enough money for bus fare. Besides, I wanted to see you. You're the only one who understands." At the threat of more tears, Holly reached for another handful of napkins. But the girl managed to find solace in a bite of her burger. "They're being so . . . so irrational!"

Holly played with her salad, trying to figure out how to give comfort without taking sides in a family argument. "Ginny, what do your parents want you to take in college?"

The girl shrugged. "Anything but petroleum engineering. I think Mom would like to see me become a nurse or a teacher or something like that. You know, a traditional female role."

"My brother is a teacher, and I know a very handsome male nurse. His female patients love him."

"Men like that are the exceptions," Ginny said with her mouth full. "I want to be something different, something challenging."

"If you don't think teaching is challenging you've never been in my brother's civics class."

The girl washed down some french fries with a swallow of coke. "Whose side are you on?"

Holly sighed. "No one's, honey. I just hate to see you fight with your parents like this." Ginny seemed too preoccupied with the rest of her meal to answer, so Holly sat for a moment thinking. One of Ginny's comments had planted the germ of an idea.

"When you're finished, why don't I show you around the rig?" she suggested. "In a few years you're going to be spending a lot of time out here, so you might as well get the feel of things."

Ginny perked up immediately. "Oh, I'd love that."

Holly checked Ginny into the company office, then took her young friend on a thorough round of the platform. Starting on the bottom deck, they saw a few crewmen fishing and diving from the gangplanks.

"Those ropes are neat," Ginny commented, pointing to the knotted hawsers which the men used to pull themselves out of the water.

"They're a lot more then neat when a worker falls into the water or we need them to slide down in case of an emergency," Holly told her. "But they are fun to use during off-hours."

Moving to the next deck, they went through the noisy banks of compressors and engines that kept the platform running, and the rows of consoles that monitored the huge operation. Ginny looked at everything with polite interest, but Holly could see that machinery wasn't her thing.

On the next level, however, her reaction was one of astonishment. Ginny looked in wide-eyed disbelief at the room Holly shared with her five male crewmates.

"You sleep *here?*" she asked, dumbfounded. "You mean they don't supply you with your own cabin?"

"There's no room, Ginny. Women working out here are treated very much the same as men. Come on, I'll show you my one big luxury."

Holly led Ginny to a tiny storeroom where they had to pick their way through stacks of supply boxes. At the back of this room another door led into a small, very cluttered bathroom. "This is the ladies' room," she said proudly, switching on the single, stark light-bulb above the sink.

Ginny looked at her friend as if she'd lost her mind. "This?" Her youthful eyes took in even more boxes piled on either side of the sink, the less than clean floor and the depressing green walls. "But this is . . . this is . . ."

"The only privacy I've got on board this rig, honey. And believe me, I treasure it. Since I'm the only woman on the rig I have to share it with a few boxes and bottles of soap. But given the alternative, I'm not complaining."

Ginny said little as they finished the tour with a walk around the main deck of the platform. When Holly showed her the drilling rig with all its pipe, bags of mud powder and other paraphernalia, the girl looked awed.

"I had no idea that a platform looked like this," she said as they returned to the cafeteria for another coke and coffee. "It's so noisy and crowded, and well, grimy."

"It is that." Holly sipped her coffee, easily reading Ginny's disappointed expression. She'd seen the same look on other visitors who'd come aboard. For some reason, offshore oil rigs frequently didn't live up to people's expectations.

When they were through with their drinks, Holly insisted that Ginny call her parents and tell them she was all right. Expecting an argument, she was a little surprised when the girl made no protest. She was even more astounded when Ginny told her she was ready to return to shore. Happy to leave well enough alone, Holly didn't question her. But because an afternoon wind had come up, she did ask one of the roughnecks who was waiting to go ashore with the supply ship to accompany Ginny back in the power-boat.

"Thanks for listening to me," the girl said, giving Holly a quick hug and kiss.

"I'm sorry I wasn't more help."

"There's not a lot you can do," Ginny said. She gave her friend a final squeeze. "And you did help, honest. I've got . . . well, I've got a lot to think about."

The next morning Holly watched Kirk and Larry Rees enter the diving bell just as the first fragile rays of sunlight touched the glittering steel platform. She was up earlier than she needed to be, and after making several inane comments to herself about the early bird getting more work done, she finally admitted she'd sacrificed her sleep simply to get one more glimpse of Kirk before he went below.

Holly stood at the rail until the bell was out of sight, reminded herself that worry and work on an oil rig do not mix, then spent the next hour trying to practice her own preaching. The results were not a spectacular success.

Shortly before seven, a prickly sense of *déjà vu* penetrated Holly's concentration. Just as before, she was suddenly aware of an increased level of activity going on around the decompression chamber. One look at Butch Kelley's face and her heart lurched terribly. Rushing over, she heard him yell into the communications line.

". . . don't bother to analyse it, man. Get him back to the bell. If it's the high pressure seat he's probably out of air by now. Get moving!"

"Butch, what is it?" Holly's voice was so strained she could hardly hear it over the noise of the rig. Kelley seemed to look right through her as he turned to Don Cassill.

"The minute they get back in that bell get it up here fast! Rees wasted too damn much time fiddling with the regulator. I don't know how long he's been without air."

"*Who's* without air? For God's sake, what's happening down there?"

Kelley dismissed her irritably. "Not now. We've got an emergency."

"Damn it, I know you've got an emergency." Holly knew she was near tears and bit her lip to hold them back. More controlled, she went on, "Did something happen to one of the air tanks?"

Kelley spat out something Holly couldn't catch and once again depressed the mike button, twisting away from her so she could no longer hear what he was saying. In desperation, she turned to Don Cassill. "Don, tell me what's going on."

The young diver's tanned face glistened with perspiration. "Roberts signaled he was having trouble with his air tank. When Rees went to assist, Roberts pointed to his regulator. That's all we know."

"But has Rees gotten him back to the bell?" Holly's heart was pounding so hard now she had to hold onto the side of the chamber for support. Kirk was in trouble! His life might be in danger down there and there wasn't one damn thing she could do to help!

Cassill shook his head, adding to Holly's fears. "We don't know that yet, either." Seeing how worried she was, he patted her awkwardly on the shoulder. "Listen, Rees would do anything for Roberts. And that includes going to any lengths to get him back here in one piece."

Holly nodded, but her hands clenched and unclenched in nervous frustration as she went back to listening to Kelley's conversation with the divers.

"Okay, get the door open," Kelley was saying into the mike. His voice was more controlled now, but Holly could see that the sweat on his face had started to roll onto his neck and down his shirt. "Never mind his helmet now. Every damn minute counts! Get him in that bell and then take it off."

Kelley jerked around and told Cassill, "Tell those medics to be standing by the minute that bell gets up here. And tell them to have emergency oxygen ready."

Holly watched Kelley spit a few more words into the mike, then stood by as he motioned for the men on the giant crane to pull up the bell. "Is he going to be all right?" she asked him, unable to imagine what she would do if the answer were no. Kirk was too vital to die, too audacious, too alive!

Now that there was nothing to do but wait, Kelley finally acknowledged her presence. "I don't know," he told her bluntly. "Rees says something went wrong with Roberts's regulator. If the high pressure seat exploded like the kid thinks, then the tank probably emptied in less than a minute. You can't breathe air that fast, lady." He made a helpless gesture with his hands. "We won't know until they get back up how bad it was."

So with the rest of the crew, Holly once again went through the agony of waiting—eyes glued below, watching for the diving bell to break the surface of the ocean. The wind had come up in the past hour, and the water beat restlessly against the platform, seeming to match the churning state of her emotions. He had to be all right, she told herself, and the words repeated themselves again and again to form a silent rhythm with the sea. He had to be all right. He *would* be all right!

An eternity later the steel bell glinted in the water, rising slowly until it reached the deck. As before, Kelley supervised while the bell was attached to the deck decompression chamber. As before, the medics entered the chamber laden with their supplies and their skills. As before, Holly died, inch by inch, minute by minute, as she awaited word of his condition. Only this time it was longer, much longer, before Kelley's craggy face lit in a relieved grin.

"He's okay!" he shouted over the whine of machinery and wind. "By God, he's gonna be good as new! Takes more than a bad regulator to stop a guy like Kirk Roberts!"

This time there was no strength left in Holly to make

it to the dining room. Stepping almost blindly around a pile of pipes that were stored a short distance from the decompression chamber, she sank quietly to the deck. The sobs she had withheld before were released now, and her shoulders shook uncontrollably, as much from relief as from the terrible fear that had taken possession of her heart and mind.

He was safe. Thank God he was safe!

Holly put her head between her knees and sucked in deep breaths of air, willing back her control. It was over, and yet it would never be over. As long as he continued to play this incessant game with fate it would never end. How many more times could she watch him go down only to wonder if he would live to come up? How much more punishment could his body stand?

Holly looked out at the endless vista of sea, at the rolling, agitated heaving of the blue-green water—aquamarine, just like his eyes. How much more punishment could *she* stand? she asked herself. How much more did she want to stand?

8

Later that afternoon, Kirk strapped on a fresh tank, complete with new regulator, and went on with the aborted dive. Since he was still under pressure, Holly didn't see him before he went back down. Which was just as well. If she'd seen him she would have either screamed at him for being so foolhardy as to go on down there again, or cried because she was petrified he wouldn't return. Since neither response was appropriate, she was almost relieved that the meeting was impossible.

Three days later she stepped onto the helicopter and flew back to Morro Bay. Behind her she left Kirk and Larry Rees resting in the deck chamber, while Kelley and Don Cassill took their turn below. Holly had heard from Carl that the dive was scheduled to continue for another two to three days. She told herself she no longer cared.

On her first day back at the aquarium, Josie diligently poked holes through Holly's carefully constructed wall of defense. "Sure you don't care," she'd told her. "And Norm's coming back any day with the Chrysler and my share of our bank accounts." Josie crushed her cigarette out with a vengeance that showed the depth of her feelings on the matter. "If there's one person you can't fool with that line, lady, it's me. I've tried to pull it too many times myself. And believe me, I cared."

"That's a first. Or maybe I should say that's the first time you've been able to make that admission sober."

"There are some things a woman would rather not admit," Josie had told her, "drunk or sober. But I sure as hell hate to see you make the same mistakes I did."

"I already made the mistake, Josie," she said. "But I'm getting out before it gets any worse."

Holly didn't go back to the aquarium after that. At night she laid awake trying to convince herself that stopping things now was better then going through the inevitable pain later. Then the pain grew almost unbearable and another little voice asked just how much worse she thought it could get? She cursed herself for her weakness and spent the next few days moping about her apartment and avoiding Josie's calls.

Ironically, Sid Hohlman was at least partially responsible for luring her out of her shell. Hauling a basket of clothes up from the laundry room one afternoon, she found him waiting at her door.

"Mr. Hohlman! What in the world are you doing here?"

"You haven't been answering your phone," he accused her. "I've been trying all week to reach you."

"I'm sorry," she lied. "My phone must be out of order," she added, compounding the fiction.

"Here, let me take that for you," he said, belatedly reaching for her laundry basket. It wasn't until after she'd relinquished her clothes that Holly realized she'd just given Sid Hohlman an entree into her apartment. Ungraciously, she unlocked the door and led him into the living room.

"Very nice," he said, looking around the homey room. "You've done a good job with the place."

Holly took the clothes and put them down on the floor. "Thank you," she said, giving her voice all the finality she could muster. "But I really don't have time to talk now."

Hohlman ignored her and deposited his heavy frame on the couch, causing the springs to squeak in protest. He patted the seat next to him. "Sit down, my dear. What I have to say will only take a few moments."

Holly sat gingerly on the arm of the overstuffed chair. Maybe if she let him talk he'd leave. "What is it you want to tell me, Mr. Hohlman?"

"Sid, my dear. After all, we're hardly strangers."

Hohlman's wink was so graphic, Holly wished they were not only strangers but living at opposite poles. Just get rid of him, she told herself firmly. Smile, be nice, but for God's sake get him out of here.

Holly gritted her teeth and said, "All right, er, Sid."

Once again he patted the seat next to him and she almost groaned. Now what, Holly? How do you get out of this one? Holly literally clamped her teeth together to suppress the words which were aching to get out, pulled her lips into the closest facsimile of a smile she could manage and moved next to him on the couch.

Holly realized her mistake immediately. Before she sank halfway into the cushion he was all over her, clumsily clawing at her breasts, his panting lips searching for her mouth.

Holly pressed her hands between them and tried to stand up. "Mr. Hohlman, please! Stop—"

Almost miraculously, considering his ineptness, Hohlman's lips fastened onto hers and held, the hard, moist kiss nearly causing her to gag. With no discernable technique other than to stay the distance, his mouth continued to grind into hers, his eager groans as repulsive to her ears as his touch was to her mouth. Holly hardly knew which to battle first, the hands that seemed to be everywhere, or the mouth that refused to let go.

When his fingers pinched crudely at her breasts, the question was quickly settled. Raising her right knee as far as possible considering the cramped circumstances, she kicked hard into the ample roll of his stomach. The results were prompt and gratifying. Recoiling, Hohlman clutched at his middle, his eyes wide and accusing.

"Why you little—" Releasing one of the hands holding his abdomen he reached out for her, but Holly was already across the room.

"Get out!" she told him, positioning herself next to the telephone. "Get out of here and don't come back!"

He was standing now, but his hands were still holding his stomach as he started toward her.

"I said get out, Mr. Hohlman. Or by God I'll call for help." She placed her hand on the phone; regional manager or not, she was ready to use it. Hohlman looked at the hard set of her mouth and stepped back. With unsteady hands he made a belated attempt to straighten his clothes.

"There's no need to do that, Holly, er, Miss Bishop," he said, his tone a placating whine. "There's obviously been a misunderstanding. When you invited me in, then sat so close to me on the couch, well, what's a man to think?"

His weak, slightly off center grin was as sickening as the rest of his performance, a fitting end to the visit. "I don't give a damn what you think," she hissed, not bothering to argue. "Just get out of here. Now!"

He drew himself up to his full five-foot-nine-inch height and looked at her levelly. "All right, I'll leave," he told her. "But I promise you I won't forget this episode. If I were you I'd watch my step very closely, Miss Bishop. Very closely indeed."

After he'd gone, Holly went on a rampage scouring her apartment. It was as if by cleaning her home she could cleanse herself of the man who had so crudely attempted to soil her body. When she was finished she had exhausted most of her physical frustrations, but the mental disgust stayed with her throughout dinner. She hadn't heard the end of the matter; Hohlman's parting threat had been warning enough of that.

Holly spent the rest of the evening trying to puzzle out his intentions, but it was impossible. There was no doubt he could make things very difficult for her on the job. But could he actually get her fired?

Much later, when Holly finally fell into a troubled sleep, she was no closer to finding an answer than she'd been before.

Holly awakened the next morning to the sound of firecrackers and the rousing blare of a marching band. Going sleepily to the window, she looked out to find dozens of people hurrying in the direction of the boulevard. Holly pulled up the sash and listened to the beat of drums and cymbals. It wasn't just one band, it was several. It was a parade!

By the time she'd turned the heat on under the coffee pot, Holly had awakened enough to realize that it was the Fourth of July. It was easy to forget the date when you worked seven days straight on an offshore oil rig. This time, because of Kirk, her mind had been even more preoccupied than usual. The town was having a party. And from the sound of it, every man, woman and child in the city had turned out for the festivities.

Except her! Suddenly Holly had an urge to join in the fun. If she stayed home today she'd just worry about Sid Hohlman, or worse, mope about Kirk. It was time to get both men out of her mind. And what better way to forget than to help Morro Bay celebrate the nation's independence?

Humming to herself, Holly quickly showered then pulled on a white cotton, full-skirted dress, with a scoop neck decorated in bright yellow and orange daisies. Brushing her long dark hair until it shone, she hurried back to the kitchen and threw some leftover chicken, hard-boiled eggs, pickles, potato chips and cookies into a lunch hamper. As an afterthought, she tossed in some paper napkins and a blanket, then knotted a sweater around her neck and ran downstairs to join the crowd headed for the boulevard.

After the parade came a pie-eating contest, the three-legged and sack races, and the world championship oyster shucking and eating contest. Holly watched fascinated as the teams—one shucker and one eater—went through an unbelievable pile of oysters before one of the teams was declared the winner and offered a large glass of bicarbonate of soda. The town roared when the eating member of the team gratefully accepted it.

After eating her picnic lunch, Holly strolled along a colorful line of food and game booths, and realized she was feeling surprisingly relaxed. She was happier than she'd been in days; she felt part of the community, and it reminded her of other, earlier July Fourths when she was growing up in Gilroy. People she hardly knew greeted her with such open smiles that she finally concluded the citizens of Morro Bay had decided to bury the oil-issue hatchet, at least for the duration of the holiday.

She was wandering through the Morro Bay Art Association's "Art in the Park" exhibit, when she came across Ginny Palermo and her parents. Remembering her meeting with Mario Palermo aboard the oil rig, Holly wasn't sure how the fisherman would react to seeing her again, especially in light of his daughter's decision to become a petroleum engineer. It was a pleasant surprise when the man not only enthusiastically pumped her hand, but also introduced her to his wife, Rose.

Mrs. Palermo was short and slender, and Holly could see where Ginny had inherited her beautiful, doe-like brown eyes. The woman smiled at her warmly.

"At last I meet the great Holly Bishop," Rose Palermo told her. "Ginny talks about you all the time. You've made quite an impression on her, you know."

Holly returned her smile self-consciously, aware that Ginny's admiration for her had been at least partly responsible for the family's recent problems. "I'm very pleased to meet you, Mrs. Palermo. Ginny's told me a lot about you, too."

"And lately not much of it was good, I'll bet." The

woman's hearty laugh took any possible sting out of the words.

Sensing Holly's confusion, Ginny said, "I've enrolled for college—at the University of Santa Barbara. Isn't it exciting?"

"Yes, of course," Holly said hesitantly. "But I don't—"

"I'm going to major in oceanography, Holly," Ginny said, laughing at her friend's bewilderment. "You know, the study of the ocean's environment—the animals and the plants and all that stuff. It's so close to what I've been doing at the aquarium, I don't know why I didn't think of it sooner." She looked sheepishly at her friend. "It wasn't until you showed me around the oil rig the other day that I realized that wasn't the kind of life I wanted at all. Until then, I guess I just didn't understand what a petroleum engineer did."

Holly smiled, relieved she wasn't going to be tarred and feathered after all. "A lot of people don't, Ginny. That's why it's good to see a job firsthand before you spend years studying for it." She hugged the girl. "I'm so happy it's finally settled."

"*You* are!" Rose Palermo said with another of her infectious laughs. "Listen, it's no fun being the villain. And we can bend a little when we have to. Ginny's convinced us that Santa Barbara has one of the best oceanography courses on the West coast. And if our daughter's going to work with fish and seaweed for the rest of her life, she'd better know what she's doing." The woman took Holly's arm. "Say, why don't you join us for dinner? We're going to have a barbecue with a group of our friends. Then later we can watch the fireworks together. For a small town, Morro Bay puts on a pretty good show."

To Holly's consternation, the Palermo's group of friends turned out to be most of the Morro Bay Fishermen's Association. Feeling something like the Trojan horse, she awkwardly suffered through dozens of introductions, then found she couldn't remember a single name five minutes later. If she was nervous, it was obvious that the fishermen and their families were dumbfounded to discover a member of the enemy camp in their midst, and invited for dinner, at that.

None of them had counted on Rose Palermo. With a *sangfroid* which would have been the envy of many a Washington politician, Ginny's mother soon calmed the charged atmosphere. By the time the steaks were ready, Holly was even discussing the inevitable oil lease with the men, but this time there was no antagonism, just mutual sympathy and respect.

"So what you're saying is that Worldwide doesn't pay enough attention to your complaints," she summarized over homemade cake and ice cream. "You know I just didn't realize that our pipes were interfering with your fishing nets."

"Yet we've told the company office that time and time again," Mario Palermo told her. "A move of just five hundred feet would get them out of our fishing lanes."

Holly listened as several of the other men added suggestions or ideas of their own, and as she did, an idea began to grow. "If I could arrange for you to meet regularly with representatives of the company, would you be willing to arbitrate your grievances there?"

"Not if Sid Hohlman's included," one of the men said.

"He doesn't listen," another complained. "He just makes excuses, or promises he never keeps."

Holly refrained from adding what else Sid Hohlman

did, and said, "What if you had some say in the board's composition?"

"We'd have to put it to a vote," Mario said cautiously. "But off the record, I think it's a great idea!"

The rest of the fishermen seemed to agree, and as Holly looked around at the hopeful smiles she wondered what she'd gotten herself into. The day before Sid Hohlman had told her to watch her step and here she had all but promised to go over his head on behalf of the fishermen.

This is not going to be easy, she told herself grimly. You have just agreed to pull one very slippery rabbit out of the hat. But whatever the risks, or her chances of succeeding, Holly decided the end result was important enough to give it a damn good try. She would just have to worry about Sid Hohlman's threats later.

The fireworks started shortly after dark. By now Holly was feeling comfortable enough with the Palermos and their friends to add her cheers to theirs as each successive burst seemed to outdo the one before. Holly was so absorbed in the display that she was hardly aware when someone dropped beside her on the blanket.

"Strange company you keep," a low voice murmured in her ear. "Usually when an oil engineer sits down with a fishermen's group it's to start fireworks, not to watch them."

"Kirk!" When several of her new friends looked at her curiously, she lowered her voice. "What are you doing here?"

"Enjoying the Fourth of July. Just like you." He looked around at the Palermos and the other fishermen's families. "What are you doing sitting here in the middle of the enemy camp—and looking as if you're having a damn good time?"

"The Palermos invited me. And we *are* having a good time." Belatedly, Holly remembered her resolution concerning Kirk, and added a little more harshly, "Any law against that?"

She saw the quick, questioning look that crossed his face. "Touchy tonight, aren't we? I thought after so long without seeing me you'd give me a better greeting than that."

She saw the hunger on his face and wondered how she was ever going to resist him. But when he leaned over for the expected kiss, she turned away, pretending to look at another bright shower of sparks overhead. Holly heard his surprised grunt, but said nothing. After several strained moments, she felt his hand on her arm.

"Come on," he said.

"Kirk, let go of my arm. I'm not going anywhere until the fireworks are over."

"Lady, the fireworks are just about to begin." His grip on her arm tightened and Holly knew she either had to go with him or risk a scene. Turning to Mrs. Palermo, she quickly made her goodbyes, thanking the woman for everything.

"I should be the one doing the thanking," the woman replied. "Both for Ginny and for listening to these good-for-nothing fishermen of mine." Her dark eyes sparkled mischievously. "I had a feeling that once we got a woman involved in this we'd see some action."

"I'll do everything I can," Holly told her. "I can't promise anything definite, but I'll do my best."

Mrs. Palermo gave her a little hug. "I know you will, dear. And I wish you luck."

Kirk led her to the cocktail lounge of a nearby waterfront restaurant. Because of the fireworks, the place was nearly deserted, and neither Kirk nor Holly noticed the well-dressed man quietly drinking gin and tonics in a corner booth. But the man noticed them, and as they crossed the room toward a window seat overlooking the bay, he shrunk even further into the shadowed recesses of his compartment.

Sid Hohlman watched with interest as they ordered drinks, wishing he were close enough to hear what they were saying. But he was afraid to move for fear of drawing attention to himself. Instead, he raised his hand slightly and motioned for the waitress to refill his drink. Then he settled back to watch the drama by the window, thanking whatever lucky stars had led him to this restaurant and presented him with the chance he'd been waiting for.

"Okay, what's this all about?" Kirk looked at her across the table and thought how beautiful she was by candlelight. Already his body ached for her even as his mind told him he had to settle whatever was bothering her first. Had she found someone else, he wondered? That was one of the problems with his line of work; women were seldom happy to see their man only once or twice a week, if that. Only he hadn't pegged Holly Bishop as the kind of woman who would get bored and fool around. Just the opposite. She was the kind who was usually ready to wait, hoping he'd settle down. Was that it? Was she angling for a marriage proposal? And why, for the first time in his life, was that idea actually beginning to sound good?

Holly fingered her drink, searching for the words to explain her feelings. It had been so much easier when she'd rehearsed it in her mind. Now that he was sitting across from her, looking far too handsome with his blond hair and turquoise eyes, it was infinitely harder.

"It just won't work, Kirk," she said finally. "When you ran into problems during that last dive I thought . . . I thought you wouldn't . . ." She hesitated, finding it impossible to put the fear she'd experienced into words.

"You thought I wouldn't come up alive, is that it?" Kirk seemed relieved rather than put off by her explanation. "Is that all? Honey, I thought it was something serious. You really had me going there for a while."

"Kirk, it is serious. How much more serious can you get?"

Once again she saw honest confusion on his face. "But I was all right, Holly. Sure, I ran into some trouble. But there was no harm done."

Holly shook her head and her dark hair tumbled gently around her shoulders. "You don't understand, Kirk. I don't want to go through it again. I can't live like that." She looked into those blue-green eyes, wondering if she would ever be able to look at the sea again without thinking of him. "I care about you too much to go on this way, knowing that every dive you take may be your last."

"Holly, are you trying to say you love me?" The words were spoken softly, but there was an intensity in his eyes which demanded an honest answer.

She took a long sip of her wine and nodded, aware there was no more reason to hide the truth. Her feelings toward him no longer made any difference. Love alone could not make a future for them. "I love you too much to watch you risk your life day after day. You're in love with danger, Kirk. You thrive on the excitement and the travel, and all the other trimmings that go with the job." She paused a moment before she added, "I'm not sure there's room for a woman in your life."

Kirk studied his drink. "Maybe that's one of the reasons I've shied away from commitments—or maybe it just hasn't mattered until now. I know some of my reasons for getting into diving were wrong. But I've gone beyond that now. It's my life—it's all I know."

"But how much longer, Kirk?"

"How much longer will I sleep, and eat and breathe? The tide doesn't end for me. It just goes on and on. And I've been caught up in it for too long now to get free."

"But no one's locked into a lifestyle, Kirk. It's never too late to change."

His hand closed on her clenched fingers. "I wish you were right, honey. But I made a decision a long time ago and now that decision has become part of me. I don't know if I can change."

Holly didn't know how to answer, how to argue with logic that seemed totally illogical. Was perpetual danger addicting, she wondered, like drugs or alcohol? Was death the only way out of the trap for Kirk? She shook her head. "I don't understand, Kirk. I just don't understand."

"Not many people do. I wish I could make you understand. I wish I could find the words to tell you what it feels like down there." His eyes had come alive as he tried to explain, taking on a luminescence she could only envy. She was shocked to realize that for the first time in her life she hated the sea. How did you fight that kind of mistress—and win?

"You don't need the words," she told him. "It's all there in your eyes. And I don't know how to compete with it, Kirk. It's too powerful for me."

His hand tightened on her fingers. "You don't have to compete, honey. There's room for both of you in my life. Just don't ask me to give it up. I'm not sure you'd want the kind of man I'd be without it."

And I can't live with the kind of man you are *with* it, Holly thought sadly. Looking into his face, she wondered how she had ever let her feelings get so far out of hand. She had wanted him so desperately she had allowed herself to forget how many obstacles stood in their way.

"I don't want you to give up anything for me, Kirk," she said, and realized this was the truth. He was right, she wouldn't want him to change for her. If he did he wouldn't be the same man she had fallen in love with. On the other hand she knew she wasn't strong enough to stand by waiting for the end.

"So," she said too brightly, "when will you be finished on Kathy?"

"You're changing the subject, Holly." There was an awkward silence between them while the waitress brought fresh drinks.

Holly took a long sip of her wine and said, "I'm not changing the subject, Kirk. We were talking about your diving. I just wondered how long it would be until you took off again. As drilling engineer I have a right to a progress report."

"Another week or so." He took a long drink. "We're almost through with the under structure. The last thing I want to do is to check all the anodes."

"And then you're off." She swirled her wine thoughtfully. Keep your mind on the little circles,

Holly. Don't think about when he'll be gone. You knew it was going to happen. Don't get cold feet now.

"Then I'm off," he repeated.

"What's it to be?" she asked lightly. "Pyramids or *jai lai?*"

"Neither. We're headed back to the North Sea."

Holly felt as if a cold hand had been clamped over her heart. The North Sea—the most treacherous offshore duty in the world. And with the highest diver mortality rate. How long could he continue to tempt fate and come out the winner? "A glutton for punishment, huh?" she said, making the liquid circles so big they threatened to slosh over the sides.

Kirk shrugged. "Something like that. The money's good. And no one else will take the job."

"Except Kirk Roberts and company." She gulped down what remained of her wine and tipped the glass to him in a mock salute. "Three cheers for guts and raw courage."

Kirk drained his own glass and threw some bills on the tray. "Come on," he told her, taking her arm.

"You know this is getting to be a habit, Mr. Roberts," she told him. "You really have to stop ordering me around like this. How will I be able to think for myself when you're gone?"

"It's all this independent thinking of yours that's got me worried." He led her outside into the brisk night air, too preoccupied to notice that the man in the booth also rose and hastily paid for his drinks. "We'll take my car," Kirk told her.

"Where are we going?" she asked him when they'd driven a few minutes. The question was perfunctory. She knew very well where they were headed.

"Your apartment's in the next block."

She sighed. "I know. But I hadn't planned for you to go there with me tonight."

He glanced at her as he stopped the car. The low scoop neck of her dress clung provocatively to her rounded breasts and he could see the increased rate of her breathing as she followed the direction of his gaze. She had never looked lovelier, or more vulnerable. And he had never wanted her more desperately.

For a moment Kirk wondered if he was being fair to her, asking her to give so much when he had so little to give in return. He couldn't change; he wasn't even sure if he wanted to change. He ran his fingers lightly through the soft strands of her hair. But she felt so damn good. Surely one more night wouldn't hurt.

"It's what I had planned all along," he told her quietly. "I need you so badly, honey. Can't we forget about tomorrow? Just for tonight?"

"Just for tonight?" Holly nearly laughed, but it wouldn't have been appropriate because there was nothing funny in the way she was feeling. His fingers were sending all the wrong sensations to all the wrong parts of her body. Just for tonight could she forget everything that stood between them; could she forget that Kirk Roberts lived on borrowed time, that he could never settle down, that Holly Bishop needed a good deal more than that from a relationship—from life? Just for tonight could she act like someone else, someone who wasn't bothered by all those things? She shouldn't. Every ounce of common sense cried out that she was only making matters worse.

But he needed her, and she needed him. And suddenly that was enough—just for tonight.

As they went upstairs, neither of them noticed the man in the three-piece suit who took up a position in the doorway of the apartment building across the street. Nor did they think to look out either of the front-facing windows as they pulled the drapes and turned out the lights.

Across the street, Sid Hohlman settled himself into the dark opening and prepared to wait.

9

⸻⸺⦿⦿⦿⦿⦿⦿⦿⦿⦿⦿⸺⸻

They came together with a need born of desperation, neither of them willing to think any more of the
future. Tonight was here, and it was all they had.
Eagerly they clutched at it and made it theirs.

Gently, Kirk lowered the delicate white bodice of
her dress, then let his hands roam with a new kind of
urgency over her body.

"A man could get lost in all this softness, Holly," he
murmured. "And he wouldn't even care if he was
found."

He crushed her against him. His strong hands
cradled her face and his lips brushed away the tears
which glistened in her blue-gray eyes. "It's all right,
honey," he whispered. "It's all right now."

His mouth came down on hers with an impact that
left her dizzy. He felt her quiver in his arms and then
she seemed to melt, as if she were surrendering at last

to the fire that was always ready to flame to life between them.

"That's it," he murmured, letting his lips touch all the warm, golden places he had dreamed about for so many days. "I need you so much, Holly. I've thought about this for so long."

His eyes went over the lovely curve of her breasts, the nipples a warm dark rose, the skin creamy soft and inviting. Then his hands cupped their fullness, his thumbs lazily circling the tips until they flowered with desire. Her eyes were closed now, but the tears that had welled up there a moment before were trickling down her cheeks.

"Hey, why the tears?" he asked, holding her tightly in his arms. His hand stroked her hair as if she were a small child. "Honey, why are you crying?"

"Because I'm an idiot!" she sobbed. "Because my body wants you and my mind wants you and it's all wrong and I don't . . . I don't know what to do about it. I've tried to fight it and I can't."

He continued to stroke her silken hair, and the quiet strength of his body calmed and reassured her. "You don't want me any more than I want you," he told her, his voice deep and rich. "And fighting it just doesn't work. I know because I've tried."

He bent his head and kissed away each tear, and Holly thought she had never experienced anything so sweet. All the while he was murmuring softly, his words muffled in her cheek and hair and neck, but the sounds soothing her nonetheless. And then, just when she thought she would go crazy from her need for him, his lips touched hers, so softly, so slowly, that the kiss was barely more than a whisper. Without thinking she moved her body, lightly rubbing her hips against his, her bare breasts touching the cool material of his shirt. She sighed. It felt good—so very, very good.

"You feel . . ." his voice sounded strained ". . . you feel absolutely marvelous." Quickly he jerked open the buttons on his shirt so that her breasts came in contact with the golden hair that covered his chest. "Would you like to go through that routine again? I didn't quite catch it all the first time."

Holly chuckled deep in her throat and happily obliged. This time when she moved against him she was shocked by the hard, throbbing proof of his desire.

"I don't know where you learned to do that, Holly, but I approve. Lord, do I approve."

Unable to wait any longer, Kirk picked her up and carried her to the bedroom and laid her on the bed. He tried to keep the anticipation out of his fingers as he pulled her dress over her hips and down her long, beautiful legs, but he was too eager to be gentle. He had to see her naked again. He had to possess her totally.

When finally she lay naked beneath him, his eyes traveled hungrily over the softly rounded length of her. "Do you know how many hours I've spent thinking of you, wanting to see you like this, wanting to touch you and make you mine? Divers have a lot of time to think when they're decompressing, honey. Long, boring hours when there just isn't a hell of a lot to do. And lately I've spent just about all that time thinking about you." Quickly, he stripped off his clothes. "Tonight I intend to live out each and every one of those fantasies."

Then he let his hands touch her. Fighting for control, he let them slide over her smooth shoulders and down her arms and across the delicate, full swell of her breasts. Lovingly he tested their weight in his palms, then molded and shaped them and held them up to his eager lips. With a little groan he licked and sucked one perfectly shaped nipple.

His hands went on with their exquisite exploration, sliding smoothly over the narrow indentation of her waist, and lower to her stomach. He paused there, memorizing the small details—the tiny mole just above the silken triangle of hair, the way her tan contrasted with this small patch of lighter skin, the way she trembled at his touch.

"Please, Kirk . . . please!" She was writhing beneath him and he could feel the fire building inside her. Quickly, he withdrew his hand.

"Yes, darling. Yes. I can't wait either."

Then his knee moved between her thighs and she spread her legs eagerly for him and they were united in an embrace as old as time. He filled her completely, and her velvety softness surrounded his hardness. Again and again he plunged into her, needing to feel her, to possess her, to extinguish the flames which were consuming them both.

The end came much too quickly. But there was no holding it off. There was no way to prevent the wave after wave of ecstasy that poured over him, eliminating what little remained of his tenuous control.

But she was with him, her legs twisted tightly about his hips. Her passion matched his and her cries drove him on, making him plunge deeper and deeper. He felt a fierce elation when she called out his name, and then he was lost to everything but the explosion of his own body. Like one of tonight's fireworks displays, Kirk felt as if he were breaking apart in midair, bursting into millions of crazy, glittering pieces. He pulled her hips tightly into his, thrusting one last time into the depths of her fire, and together they soared over the top and into the calm valley that lay serenely waiting on the other side of passion.

Much later, Kirk vaguely remembered shifting his weight off her and cradling her in the crook of his arm, feeling her long dark hair splayed about their shoulders like silk. And then there was nothing until morning, and for once the dreams of holding her and loving her didn't come. He had lived out the fantasy and he was at peace. He could sleep content in the arms of the woman who said she loved him.

Outside the apartment, the weary man in the doorway shivered and pulled his thin jacket more tightly about his chest. It was after midnight and he was cold and he was tired. But he would wait.

Sid Hohlman shivered again, but it did nothing to diminish the self-satisfied smile that was just visible in the dim streetlight. Yes, he would wait, he told himself. He looked up at the darkened windows of Holly Bishop's apartment. If necessary, he would wait all night.

Kirk took the early helicopter back to the platform the next morning, and once again Holly felt bereft when he was gone. She went back to the aquarium and worked with a vengeance that alarmed Josie.

"At the rate you're going there won't be anything left for the rest of us to do around here," she told her that afternoon when Holly refused to take a lunch break. "You're a volunteer, remember? Volunteers aren't supposed to push themselves harder than the hired help."

"I'm trying to forget," Holly had told her friend candidly. "And I have a lot of memories."

"You must have seen Kirk last night then."

"Wipe that sickening grin off your face, Josie Hanson. It's disgusting the way your imagination runs away with you."

"Listen, lady, I haven't had this much fun with my imagination since my first husband brought home a carton of dirty movies." Josie opened a second pack of cigarettes and tapped the pack against the palm of her hand. Extracting one, she lit it with a quick snap of her lighter. "When will you see him again?"

"He went back to the rig this morning. If he's not in the middle of another saturation dive, I'll see him when I go back the day after tomorrow. But there's nothing left to talk about, Josie. It's all been said."

Josie took a long drag of her cigarette and studied Holly thoughtfully. "You know, kiddo, you've got about as bad a case as I've ever seen. And I've seen quite a few. Why don't you just marry the guy and be done with it?"

Holly sank onto the chair behind the counter. "I can't marry him. He won't change and I can't live with things the way they are. If you think I'm nervous now, you ought to see me when he goes down in that bell. His chances aren't good, Josie. One of these days the odds are going to catch up with him."

Josie sat quietly for a few minutes. "You've got a problem, all right. You can't live with him, and you sure as hell are a basket case without him." She tapped the ash from her cigarette into a nearby abalone shell. "So what are you going to do about it?"

"Josie, if I knew the answer to that one I wouldn't be sitting here going crazy. I know it's hopeless, yet I can't stop hoping. What are you going to do when your heart's breaking with love and your head's full of that kind of logic?"

One thing Holly did was to continue to keep busy.

The following day she placed a call to Worldwide Oil's corporate office in San Francisco and after hounding several secretaries, she finally managed to get through to one of the corporate managers. Succinctly outlining the fishermen's grievances, she went on to explain her idea about setting up an arbitration board to meet regularly with their local association. To her astonishment, the official seemed genuinely enthusiastic about the idea, promising to look into it immediately and to get back to her during her next seven-off.

Holly went back to the rig the next morning feeling she had at least made progress in one quarter. With any kind of luck, and some perseverence on her part, her plans for the fishermen might even be implemented.

She wished there was even a fraction of that much hope for Kirk and herself. Since his team had already commenced their final work on the rig's under structure, she didn't see him during her first two days back on the job. Even when the dive was finished she knew they would have only a day or two at best before he went down to make the final check on the anodes. And when that dive was finished they'd be gone, to the most difficult, perilous offshore drilling operation in the world. The North Sea.

Early on her third day back on the rig, Sid Hohlman flew in with the morning helicopter. The fact that his appearance happened to coincide with their finally hitting oil on the number five well did little to relieve the overdose of "Hohlrassment," as Carl dubbed the manager's constant interference. After four straight hours of unsolicited advice and criticism, Holly and Carl managed to duck down to the cafeteria for a well deserved cup of coffee.

"You must be feeling pretty pleased with yourself,"

the toolpusher said, referring to the bet they'd made weeks ago about when the well would hit oil. The coincidence of Holly guessing the event to the day was a standing joke with the crew this morning.

"I warned you not to fool around with woman's intuition, Carl," she said. "Now where's my five dollars?"

"You don't waste any time, do you?" He patted his empty pockets. "Give me a break, Holly. Danny was hotter than a pistol at the game last night. Give me until tonight to recoup."

Holly made a mock face, knowing full well that ongoing poker games were as much a part of an offshore crew's pastime as movies and homemade apple pie. She pretended to consider. "How do I know you won't skip out with the cash?"

"There's a Dolly Parton movie on tomorrow night. No way do I jump ship before that."

Holly laughed. "Okay, Carl. But only until the movie. After that, it's pay up or do my night emergency calls for a whole week."

Somehow Holly managed to make it through the rest of the day with Holhman constantly looking over her shoulder and generally behaving as if he were the only person on the rig who knew how to handle a new oil discovery. By late afternoon, his conflicting orders had succeeded in throwing the entire drilling operation behind schedule. On the way to dinner, Carl Morris was livid with anger.

"Damn it all, Holly," he snarled, using the strongest language she'd ever heard out of the normally good-natured toolpusher. "If that high-strutting, poor excuse for a company bigwig doesn't stay out of my way, so help me he's going over the side, fancy three-piece suit and all. He's got this operation so damn tangled up it's gonna take three days to get back to where we were when he got out of that helicopter this morning."

Holly tried to calm her friend, but only for the sake of his soaring blood pressure, not to help Sid Hohlman. Personally, she was finding the regional manager's visit provoking in more than one respect. The man who'd come on board this morning was subtly different from the Sid Hohlman she was used to dealing with. He was still offensive and basically stupid in the way he dealt with his subordinates, but there was an underlying difference in the way he treated her, a difference she just couldn't quite figure out.

As he sat across the table from her at dinner, she caught his eye and it finally clicked. His expression was just like the one she'd caught on Rusty Martin's freckled face the day the red-headed third grader hid a grass snake in her desk. It was an I-know-something-you-don't-know, and you're-not-going-to-like-it look. And Holly didn't like it. In fact, it very effectively destroyed her appetite, leaving her much too frustrated to eat.

The problem was, of course, that until she came upon the snake—or whatever Hohlman had in mind for her—there wasn't a damn thing she could do, either about his expression or her hunch concerning it. Going to Carl would seem silly and probably paranoid. Very likely he'd just laugh again at her "woman's intuition" and point out that Sid Hohlman was always up to something, so what else was new. But Holly was sure something was brewing behind those dark, beady little eyes. And she knew she was going to remain very uncomfortable until she discovered exactly what it was!

Kirk and his crew completed their current saturation dive just as Holly's table started on dessert. When she saw the four men come into the dining room, all thoughts of Sid Hohlman flew out of her mind. He looked tired, she thought, and pale. And there was a strain around his eyes which hadn't been there that last night he'd stayed at her apartment.

Holly watched the men heap their plates full of the cook's savory pot roast and hot, rich gravy. She knew how much the divers dreaded the long, boring hours they spent in decompression. He probably just hadn't eaten as well as he should have during the last diving operation, she rationalized.

Kirk caught her eye and winked, and the secret of that other, intimate life they shared away from the rig reached across the room to warm her heart and calm her fears. Not to worry, Holly, she told herself, he'll look better tomorrow. Four days of pressurization were bound to leave anyone looking a little drawn.

But as she left the dining room with the rest of her group, Holly did worry. She spent the rest of the evening worrying about it a great deal.

The hand shaking her arm wouldn't stop, and Holly mumbled and turned over in her sleep, willing it to go away and leave her alone. But it wouldn't go away, and the voice that accompanied the annoying intrusion, was even more persistent.

"Come on, Holly, wake up. We need you up on deck. Pronto."

Sleepily opening one eye, Holly raised her left arm and saw by the luminous dial on her digital watch that it was two o'clock in the morning. Opening the second eye, she saw Carl Morris standing by the side of her bunk. The combination sent a shot of adrenalin coursing through her body, bringing her instantly to wakefulness.

"Carl, what's the matter?"

"I'm sorry, Holly, but it's blowing a regular gale out there. One of the anodes is loose and it's banging like crazy on the rig."

Holly was already out of bed and pulling on her boots. Like most of the crew, she frequently slept in her work clothes while on the rig. There was no telling when there'd be a late night emergency, just like this one.

"You wouldn't be waking me up just because an anode came loose, Carl," she told him, catching the life jacket he tossed her. "What's the rest of the story?"

"It's the one by the electrical conductors," he told her tersely.

Holly's fingers faltered a moment as they strapped on the life vest. There was no need for Carl to explain the ramifications of the situation. Kirk and his crew had planned to examine the anodes during their last dive. In one disastrous sweep, tonight's storm had rendered that timetable obsolete. If the loose anode damaged the electrical conductor that was used to control the platform's blowout preventor, they were in serious trouble. Very serious trouble!

"When did it come loose?" she asked him as they hurried out of the cabin toward the stairs leading up to the deck.

"Near as we can figure, about an hour ago." Carl cut ahead of her to open the deck door. The gale wind hit them like a solid wall, and the toolpusher had to wrestle the door open with both hands while they fought their way outside.

"Good lord, Carl," Holly shouted above the tempest. "This is worse than I've ever seen it."

"Summer storms can be like this," the toolpusher yelled back. "Hang on to the rail or the next land you see may be Hawaii."

With a great deal of difficulty, Carl led her to the platform office, where a small, tense group was already discussing the problem. Holly was unhappy to see Sid Hohlman standing in the center of the debate, his slightly disheveled hair the only indication that he, too, had been awakened out of a sound sleep. She'd known he was planning to spend the night, he occasionally did when he thought his presence was required. But this was the first time he'd actually been around during a crisis.

"It's about time you got here, Miss Bishop," Hohlman told her icily. "That anode has to be reconnected at once, before we lose control of the wellhead."

Ignoring him, Holly turned to the other men gathered in the room. "What are our chances of holding out through the storm?" she asked them.

Quietly she listened as the men bluntly listed the odds. They weren't good. Anxiously she looked outside at the waves which were pounding into the platform with shattering force. In one respect at least, Sid Hohlman was right. If they didn't reconnect the anode they ran a very real risk of its battering the electrical conductors.

But if Kirk and his crew went down, there was an even more momentous risk to be considered. How important was a possible oil spill, no matter how severe, when measured against human lives?

"Come on, come on, Miss Bishop," Sid Hohlman said impatiently. "There's no time to be wasted. We must get the divers down there immediately!"

Holly looked around the room, stuffy now from the

smell of cigarette smoke and nervous perspiration. Every face was trained on hers, awaiting the decision that was officially hers alone to make.

Quickly, silently, Holly reviewed the options. She didn't need Sid Hohlman to tell her how important it was to reconnect the anode. On the other hand, she couldn't forget the faces of the gaunt, weary divers, one of them the man she loved. The divers had just completed four long, arduous days down there. How could she send them right back down—and in weather like this? Even if they were rested and in top physical condition, what kind of chance would they stand in this kind of weather?

"We'll wait it out," she said. "We can't send the divers down in this storm."

Several of the men nodded their heads in anxious agreement. "It's the only possible decision," Carl Morris said. "But we wanted to hear you verify—"

"It's the sentimental decision of a woman who hasn't the guts to send her lover down to do what must be done," Sid Hohlman interrupted.

Holly felt a cold chill at the vindictive look on his face. So that was it. Somehow Hohlman had found out about her and Kirk and had been waiting to use that knowledge against her.

"Of course the divers will go down," he went on, his voice brooking no argument. "We can't risk this rig and all the bad publicity that's sure to come out of another oil spill just so Miss Bishop can coddle her sweetheart." He turned to one of the crew. "Go get the divers."

"No!" Holly put a restraining hand on the man's arm. "It's my decision. And I say we'll wait it out."

"As regional manager for Worldwide Oil, I'll make

164

the decision as to what's best for the company." Hohlman's voice rose threateningly.

"Not aboard this rig you won't," Holly told him. "Out here the responsibility's mine. And I'm not going to risk four lives just because you're afraid of some bad publicity."

Holly's eyes had turned a dark gray, and she sensed her co-workers surprised admiration as she faced the manager. "Now, I'm going to have to ask that you either be quiet or leave this office, Mr. Hohlman. We have a long night ahead of us."

The manager's face suffused with anger. Turning to the same worker, he snapped, "I said get the divers."

The man shuffled uncomfortably and looked at Holly. The determination he saw on her small face seemed to be all the reassurance he needed. "I'm sorry, Mr. Hohlman, but Miss Bishop says we'll wait it out. I guess that's what we're going to have to do."

"Why you cheap, conniving little bitch!" the manager exploded, moving menacingly toward Holly. "Just because you're sleeping with that over-the-hill collection of brawn and muscle doesn't mean you're going to jeopardize my—"

Kirk's fist caught Hohlman solidly under the chin. The storm was so loud no one had heard the diver come into the office and he'd crossed the room before anyone could stop him. As if in slow motion the manager's back arched for a moment, then he went sprawling over a desk, landing hard against the opposite wall. Paper, pencils and charts went flying. A coffee cup shattered. Other than the fierce, howling wind outside, there was total silence in the room.

"Get up," Kirk told him. "Get up and apologize to Miss Bishop."

Slowly, Sid Hohlman picked himself off the floor, one hand rubbing his chin, the other steadying himself on the edge of the desk. "You're going to pay for this, Roberts," he snarled. "Both of you are going to pay."

Kirk took a step forward and the manager instinctively flinched and moved backwards. "I said apologize. Now!"

Hohlman hesitated, then when Roberts made another move toward him he said quickly, "All right, all right. I'm sorry." The look of pure hatred he directed at her made Holly want to cringe. She nodded her head silently, not trusting herself to speak, and watched Hohlman stumble from the room. When she turned, Kirk was talking earnestly to Carl Morris, the annoying little man already forgotten.

"We can be down there in half an hour. I'll take Kelley and Rees. Can you help Cassill man the on-deck mike?"

"Kirk! You can't go down there!" Holly stepped between the two men. "It's suicide. What do you think I've just been telling Hohlman?"

"Hohlman's an idiot," Kirk told her abruptly. "But he's right, the repair has to be made. That's what we're here for, Holly. It's times like these when we earn our keep."

Holly felt a surge of hysteria. "No! You can't go. I won't let you. It's crazy . . . it's . . . it's totally insane."

Gently, Kirk placed his hands on her shoulders and moved her aside. He kissed her lightly on the forehead, then began issuing orders as he strode briskly out of the room. The other men followed, ignoring Holly now that imminent action lay ahead.

When she finally followed, the divers were already suiting up in the relative shelter of the deck decompression chamber. Holly could only stand numbly by, watching as they readied themselves for what might be their last dive aboard Kathy. Their last dive anywhere!

Carl came to stand by her as the divers made a hurried check of their equipment. "I tried to talk him out of it, but he's determined to go down there. He says they can do it."

"He's crazy, Carl," she said, her words lost in the fury of the storm. "And God help him, God help us both, I hope he's right!"

As Holly watched the bell rise into the black, wrathful night, she felt a fear unlike any she'd experienced before in her life. It clutched at her heart and turned her blood to ice. And the seconds that came as the bell disappeared beneath the frothing surface were an eternity to be suffered in silent agony.

The next hour became one long prayer. Each screech of the microphone produced a new terror. Twice, two of the men became separated from the others in the black tangle of steel beneath the rig, and precious moments were spent locating them and bringing them back. Several times voice communication faltered or was temporarily lost due to the unremitting force of the storm, and toward the end of the dive it broke down altogether, bringing a collective moan from those who stood watch on the deck.

Nearly fifteen minutes later, an all but unintelligible squawk came from the independent communication system aboard the diving bell. They were ready to come up. The anode was reattached, the nightmare was nearly over.

But as Holly watched the bell come up through the sheet of rain which was now pelting the deck, she knew that for her the nightmare would never be over, not as long as she was in love with Kirk Roberts. The bell safely touched the deck, but she was already moving back toward the office, fighting against a force far more potent than the wind and rain.

Holly knew now what had to be done. And this time there would be no turning back.

10

Holly didn't see Kirk again before she left the rig at the end of the week. Instead of decompressing after their stormy, late-night descent, the men decided to extend the dive until all the anodes had been checked. But then, she would have made it a point not to see him again at any rate. Holly had just put in her last terrifying vigil. She knew she hadn't the courage to go through another.

She stayed in Morro Bay just long enough to collect her mail and call Josie, then packed up her car for the three-hour drive north to Gilroy. Holly wasn't taking any chances. She was only willing to trust her new determination so far. Kirk was sure to call before he and his crew took off for the North Sea. She didn't want to be there when he did.

As usual, the week home with her parents was like a balm to her flagging spirits, especially since the Garlic Festival was in full swing. There were some things that just didn't change, and it was this permanence that Holly clung to now while the rest of her world crumbled. She knew her mother suspected something was wrong, but typically she didn't pry. And because she didn't, Holly finally broke down on her second night at home and told her the whole story.

"You love him very much, don't you, dear?" her mother asked as they sat companionably on the front porch of the old Spanish-style house.

Holly nodded. "Too much to watch him commit slow suicide, Mom. After all this time, why did I have to go and fall for a guy like that?"

"Hearts are not noted for being particularly discriminatory, honey," her mother answered. "I guess that's where commonsense comes in."

"So you think I'm doing the right thing?"

Janet Bishop smiled. "You mean by running away?"

"I'd hardly call it running away. I just needed some time . . . some distance."

"And he'll be gone when you get back."

"Somehow when you put it that way it does sound as if I'm running." Holly sighed and pulled a leaf off one of the azalea bushes which were in vivid bloom along the front of the house. "But it doesn't make much difference whether I run or stay. It's hopeless anyway. There's no future for us."

"Oh, I don't know," her mother said softly. "Where there's love, you'd be surprised what's possible. You might be very surprised indeed."

At the end of the week, Holly had returned to Morro Bay, rested in body and at least partially healed in spirit. The first thing she found after entering her apartment were three notes from Kirk, all hand delivered and slipped under her door. With a pounding heart, she quickly ripped all three into tiny pieces before she could give in to the temptation to open them.

It's not going to be easy, she told herself, finding it equally difficult to ignore the constant ringing of the telephone. You're going to have to be strong, she thought, tossing items carelessly into the duffle bag she always brought with her aboard the rig. You're going to have to be very strong and very determined. Don't think about Kirk—forget the days you spent lazing in the sun, and the evenings you looked out over the bay, and the nights when his hands roamed all over your body—Good lord, Holly! Don't think at all!

It was a little better once she was back on the rig. The memories were there too, but long, twelve-hour days made them easier to forget.

And Holly worked hard to forget. They'd started to drill the number six well, and she threw herself into the project. After dinner she suffered through movies that were too easily forgotten, and late-night TV shows that would have coaxed snores from the staunchest insomniacs.

She took to ignoring phone messages from shore, and continued to tear up the letters in Kirk's handwriting which arrived every day. For the first time in six years of working aboard offshore rigs Holly found the food unpalatable, the work not taxing enough, and her crewmates boring. She lost five pounds, couldn't sleep worth a damn and was cranky to Carl. In the simplest of terms, she was miserable.

The one bright spot in Holly's life was Sid Hohlman's conspicuous absence from the rig. When the only explanation anyone could find for this welcome respite was Holly's defiance of him on the night of the storm, she became something of a heroine. Holly wanted to feel good about it, too. But his parting look of stark hatred that night continued to haunt her dreams along with the memory of Kirk's strong arms and gentle kisses.

Kirk wrote her one letter from the North Sea—she noted the postmark with trepidation before consigning it to the same shredded fate as his other communiqués —and then she heard nothing more from him. Holly faced up to this final severance with a kind of numb acceptance, glad that it was finally over and sick with grief that it had to end at all.

The same mail brought a letter from Harry Bergman, the corporate manager she'd spoken to about setting up an arbitration board with the fishermen. He'd looked into her suggestions and found them not only economically feasible but advantageous from a public relations point of view. The letter closed with a request that she work out the details and present them in writing to his office as soon as possible.

Holly was grateful for something concrete to occupy her mind. Meeting with Mario Palermo and some of the other fishermen, she spent long hours discussing the type of panel that would be most beneficial to the group's needs. By the end of the week, she had consolidated the ideas into a definitive plan that could be quickly and easily implemented, and put it into the mail. The next day brought a very different sort of letter from Worldwide's corporate office.

Even as Holly read the polite, formally phrased summons she wasn't really surprised. Subconsciously, she'd been waiting for it, or something like it. Unless she was very much mistaken, Sid Hohlman had finally taken his revenge.

The notice was from Worldwide's executive review board, a group of officials set up to examine and act upon a wide spectrum of company issues. Just six months ago this board had been responsible for her promotion to head chemical engineer aboard Platform Kathy. Holly wondered if now the same men would find it expedient to turn around and terminate her employment with the company.

The letter requested that she appear at Worldwide Oil's main San Francisco office at two o'clock Wednesday afternoon. At that time she would be asked to explain certain aspects of her job performance over the past few months. The particulars were not spelled out, but Holly knew without being told which areas would be under discussion.

Josie's reaction to the summons was predictable. The night before Holly's scheduled appearance the two women had dinner together, and Holly was subjected to the full force of her friend's indignation.

"You aren't going to let him get away with it, are you?" Josie demanded.

"I'm going to obey the summons. I have to," Holly replied. "But I'm going to do my darndest to defend my actions, if that's what you mean."

Josie made a disgusted sound in her throat. "And you think they'll buy your story over Hohlman's?"

Holly shrugged. "Who knows? I guess that's the chance I take."

"You don't have to take it alone, you know."

Holly's heart froze. "You mean Kirk?"

"He calls every day," her friend said, her voice softer now.

"And you told him about my going to San Francisco tomorrow."

"You didn't tell me to keep it a secret." Josie peered at the younger woman intently. "Why don't you let him help you?"

173

Holly fought to keep the anguish out of her voice, off her face. "Because there's nothing he can do. Because I've got to face this alone. Because I can't . . . I can't stand to see him again."

Impatiently, Josie lit a cigarette. "That's what I thought. You're afraid."

Holly sighed and nodded wearily, too tired to argue. "Yes, I'm afraid. Of myself, not him."

"And if you're wrong?"

"I'm not, Josie. I wish to God I were. What's the sense of opening myself to fresh pain?"

Josie shook her head but there was no real conviction in her eyes. "It's your life, lady. But I want to go on record as saying I think you're making one hell of a mistake. At a time like this you need all the friends you can get. I wouldn't want to face that review board tomorrow all by myself. It's not fair."

I don't either, Holly wanted to shout in frustration and fear. Tomorrow may spell the end to all my dreams—to everything I've worked for over the past ten years. And all because Sid Hohlman couldn't take no for an answer.

Instead, she kept her face calm, her voice level. "A lot of things in this world aren't fair, Josie," she said. "Don't worry. I'll be okay."

. But the knowledge that Hohlman would hold most of the trump cards the next day stayed with her as they paid the bill and walked the few blocks back to her apartment. Secretly, Holly wasn't at all sure she'd be okay. It was impossible to tell what tomorrow might bring.

At precisely two o'clock, Holly was shown into an impressive office behind solid mahogany doors at Worldwide Oil's corporate headquarters. The review board consisted of three men, one seated behind a huge desk, the others holding court in dark leather chairs on either side.

A moment later, Sid Hohlman entered the room and he, too, was given a seat directly facing the triumvirate. The regional manager regarded her briefly, his expression smug, and Holly realized that as far as Hohlman was concerned, this meeting could have only one possible outcome.

"A rather serious charge has been brought against you, Miss Bishop," the man behind the desk began somberly. Although she'd seen R. J. Herrington's picture any number of times in company publications, this was the first time she'd been priviledged to meet Worldwide's vice-president in charge of West Coast operations. The short, overweight man to his right she recognized as a lesser vice-president. The man to his left she had never seen before.

"According to Mr. Hohlman," R. J. Herrington went on, "a situation arose several weeks ago that jeopardized one of our most vital platform operations, one, I might add, that cost Worldwide Oil considerable time and money to get approved." He paused to thumb through some papers. "Mr. Hohlman states, and I quote, '. . . for purely personal reasons, Miss Bishop refused to deal with an on-deck emergency in a responsible and satisfactory manner,' unquote." He looked up at Holly. "Do you remember the situation I'm referring to, Miss Bishop?"

Holly nodded. "Yes, Mr. Herrington. I do."

"Then can you offer this board any explanation which might account for your actions that night?"

Holly felt four pairs of eyes on her, three of them showing polite interest, the fourth complacent self-confidence. "There's really not much to tell, Mr.

Herrington. A violent storm came up that night and the weather was simply too hazardous to risk sending down the divers."

"That wasn't the real reason at all," Sid Hohlman interrupted. "She just didn't want her precious lover to get—"

"That's enough, Mr. Hohlman," Herrington cautioned. "You'll have an opportunity to speak in a moment." He turned to Holly. "Go on, Miss Bishop."

"That's about it," Holly went on quietly. "I weighed the options and decided that it was better to risk damage to the electrical conductors than to take a chance on the divers' lives. I'd make the same decision again, Mr. Herrington. As far as I was concerned, there was no other choice."

"Of course there was no choice," Hohlman exploded. "She's so besotted with that muscle-bound Adonis she's totally incapable of making a rational decision. Why, if I hadn't felt it my responsibility to spend the night on the platform, there's no telling what damage might have resulted from her ill-considered—"

"Mr. Hohlman, please!" R. J. Herrington called out impatiently. "I said you'd have your turn in a minute. Now, please, listen quietly while Miss Bishop speaks."

"I really don't have anything else to say, Mr. Herrington. I judged the storm too dangerous to risk the divers' lives. As I say, given similar conditions today, I'd make the same decision again."

"Yet the divers *did* go down that night, didn't they?"

"Yes."

"And successfully repaired the loose anode?"

"Yes sir."

"How did that come about?" R. J. Herrington sat back in his seat, idly tapping a pencil in one hand as he awaited her answer.

Holly hesitated. How could she explain to these men that Kirk Roberts had taken a foolish and extremely dangerous chance that night? In the end it boiled down to Hohlman's word against hers. "Mr. Roberts insisted on going down. He wouldn't listen to reason."

"Or the sniveling pleas of his lovesick mistress," Hohlman threw in.

Herrington raised thick gray eyebrows at his regional manager, and said to Holly, "And no injuries resulted from the dive?"

Holly gave a silent little sigh. How could she possibly describe the violence of that storm? Unless these men had actually been out there it would be useless. "No one was hurt, Mr. Herrington. That's correct."

"Yet you still maintain that the decision you made concerning their safety was the correct one."

"Yes, sir. I do."

Mr. Herrington paused for a moment to shuffle through the papers on his desk, then went on, "Mr. Hohlman goes on to accuse Mr. Roberts of unprovoked physical attack. Is this accusation correct, Miss Bishop?"

Holly hesitated before answering. Again, unless the men had been there, it would be impossible for them to understand Kirk's anger and desire to protect her. "Mr. Hohlman said some, er, rather uncomplimentary things about me, Mr. Herrington. Mr. Roberts was only coming to my defense."

"By means of physical abuse?"

Holly lowered her head, giving the barest nod.

"Because Mr. Roberts is not employed by Worldwide Oil, but was hired solely on a contractual basis, it is not within this board's jurisdiction to take action in that matter. However, we have advised Mr. Hohlman of his constitutional right to press charges in a civil court of law if that is his choice."

Once again the vice-president consulted his notes, then cleared his throat. "We come now to a somewhat personal question, I'm afraid, but one which has direct bearing on your possible motivations that night. Miss Bishop, have you, or had you at that time, been conducting an affair with Mr. Roberts?"

"You don't have to answer that, Holly. Your personal life has absolutely nothing to do with this."

Holly whirled around to find Kirk standing in the doorway, his tall frame nearly filling the entrance. Behind him a very harassed looking secretary was wringing her hands in annoyance. "I tried to keep him out, Mr. Herrington," she cried. "But he just pushed by my desk and barged in."

"That's all right, Miss Dowling," the vice-president said. "Since Mr. Roberts seems to be a central part of the issue here, I'm just as glad he, er, dropped in." He motioned to the only available seat in the room. "Please sit down, Mr. Roberts."

Kirk looked at Holly and winked. "No thank you, Mr. Herrington. If you don't mind I'd just as soon stand. Besides, you don't have enough seats for all of us." Kirk stood aside and there was a collective gasp as more than a dozen men filed silently into the room behind him.

"Gentlemen, I'd like you to meet Mr. Mario Palermo, President of the Morro Bay Fishermen's Association, and several members of his group," Kirk told the board. "And this is Carl Morris, toolpusher aboard Kathy, and the other crew members who were present in the platform office on the night of the storm. Also, I'd like to renew your acquaintance with Mr. Harry

178

Bergman, one of your corporate managers who's been doing some business with Miss Bishop lately."

Holly joined the others in looking wide-eyed at the strange assortment of men who now filled the room to overflowing. R. J. Herrington's jaw had dropped until he was left with an expression of dumbfounded surprise, while Sid Hohlman rose from his seat as if he'd just sat on a cactus plant.

"Mr. Herrington!" he shouted. "I must protest this . . . this invasion. This is a private hearing. These people have no business in here whatsoever."

Mr. Herrington seemed to have regained some of his composure. Standing, he extended a hand to Mario Palermo and the others. "I'm sorry I can't offer you a seat," he told them apologetically, "but I had no idea—"

"You'd be invaded like this?" Kirk smiled. "You'd be surprised how many others wanted to come when they found out about this . . ." he glared at Sid Hohlman ". . . this so-called review. I understand Mr. Hohlman has lodged a complaint concerning Miss Bishop's decision on the night of the storm."

Mr. Herrington was regarding Kirk with interest. "That's correct. Do you have any information to offer?"

Sid Hohlman rose sputtering from his seat. "Why you . . . you lying, conspiring son of a—"

"Mr. Hohlman! This is the last time I care to remind you. Please sit down!"

"That's okay, Mr. Herrington, I think I've said enough. It's time the others here have a chance to say their piece." He turned to Carl Morris. "Prince, would you kindly fill the gentlemen in on exactly what happened the night of the storm?"

With a wide grin, Carl stepped forward and suc-

179

cinctly described bringing Holly to the office and the
resultant conversation concerning the safety of sending down the divers. "We all agreed it was too
dangerous," he finished. "Everyone except Mr. Hohlman here. He was all for sending them down there no
matter what the risk."

R. J. Herrington looked at the other crewmen for
confirmation. To a man, they nodded in agreement.
"And the fight?" he asked.

"Kirk took exception to Mr. Hohlman calling Miss
Bishop several very ungentlemanly names. To tell you
the truth, sir, if Kirk hadn't punched him out there
were five others in that room who would have." He
looked proudly at Holly. "Let me tell you, Mr. Herrington, Holly Bishop is one of the finest petroleum
engineers I've ever worked with, and believe me, I've
worked with the best. After just six years in the
business she knows more about drilling a well than Sid
Hohlman is likely to learn if he stays out there until
he's seventy—which we sincerely hope he won't. That
man can foul up an operation faster than any person
I've ever had the misfortune to work under."

The three-man board was regarding Holly with
renewed respect. "Then it's your considered opinion,
Mr. Morris, that Miss Bishop's decision that night was a
sound one?"

"Absolutely. It was the only possible decision under
the circumstances. To send those men down there
would have been the height of lunacy." He directed
this last comment to Hohlman.

"Thank you, Mr. Morris." The vice-president
turned to the fishermen. "And now, gentlemen, I
assume you have something to say in this matter . . ."

Half an hour later it had all been said. Mario and the

other fishermen had not minced words when it came to describing their dealings with Sid Hohlman. As far as they were concerned, he was the worst thing to come out of Worldwide Oil since the lease agreement. On the other hand, Holly Bishop, and the plans she had worked out with Mr. Bergman concerning the fishermen's arbitration board . . .

"Is my face still red? I had no idea everyone was going to have so many nice things to say about me."

Holly and Kirk were standing outside the Worldwide Building. The other goodbyes and thank yous had already been said before leaving Herrington's office. But Holly knew the final, the most painful goodbye, lay ahead.

"Honey, your face looks so good I could kiss it till sundown," Kirk told her. "And every word they said was no more than the truth. You're one of the finest things to happen to Worldwide Oil in a long, long time. To me, too," he added with a grin.

Holly didn't want to get onto that track. It was difficult enough trying to keep her few addled wits about her when he was standing this close. "Do you think they'll really fire Hohlman?"

Kirk chuckled. "If they know what's good for the company they'll send him packing so fast it'll make his little head spin. If you want my opinion, temporary suspension while the board 'investigates' his various shenanigans is much too good for him."

"I'm just grateful to clear my name."

"You did a lot more than that, honey. After what Mario Palermo and Harry Bergman said about you, I'll be surprised if you don't get a personal commendation from Worldwide's president himself."

"Thanks to you." Holly darted a quick look at him, never so happy to see anyone in her life. "How . . . how in the world did you arrange it all? You came barging in there like gangbusters!"

Kirk smiled, remembering the expression on her face when he'd burst into the room. That alone had been worth all the effort, the last minute scurry to reach everyone, to pull it off in time. "Naturally," he told her, his arms aching to feel the softness of her body. "I've always wanted to play the knight in shining armor. I haven't had so much fun in years." He gave in to the impulse to touch her arm, shivering slightly at the feel of her smooth skin. "Holly, have you any idea what you've put me through over the past four weeks? Didn't you read any of my letters?"

Holly shook her head, trying not to let him see how his touch was affecting her. "I was afraid if I read them I'd weaken. Kirk, I can only be so strong."

"Honey, if you'd read even one of those letters you wouldn't have had to be so strong, just damn quick getting back to me." Abruptly, he turned into the underground garage where he'd parked his Corvette, guiding her firmly by the arm. "We need to talk," he told her. "And I'm not about to do it standing in the middle of a San Francisco boulevard."

"But I drove in this afternoon," she protested. "My car's parked—"

"Frankly, at this particular moment I don't care where it's parked. Right now all I'm interested in is getting you where you can't run away from me." Opening the door to the sports car, he nudged her inside. "Now, are you comfortable?"

She nodded, wondering what he could possibly have to tell her that she didn't already know. Whatever it was, common courtesy demanded that she at least make an attempt to thank him for everything he'd done for her today. "I don't know how you managed it . . . this afternoon, I mean . . ." His fingers had crossed the short distance between them to stroke her hair, making it hard to concentrate. ". . . but I don't . . . I don't know how to thank you."

"We'll find a way. In fact, I've already got a couple of good ideas in mind." He leaned over and let his lips slowly cover hers. "How's that for a start, ma'am?"

Holly caught her breath. "Kirk, I don't want . . . please don't think I'm not grateful, but I just can't go through this again. It's too hard . . . it's just too hard to keep saying goodbye."

"Then why not say hello for a change?"

"You know the answer to that. There's no future for us. The tide doesn't end for you, remember? It just goes on and on. That's what you told me." Holly tried to remove the hand which was insidiously sliding beneath her blouse. "I can't go on like that. I wish I could, but I love you too much."

"Hmmm. Did you know that those words are pure music to my ears? You can't imagine the games a mind can play. When you didn't return my calls or answer my letters, I thought you'd found someone else. Where'd you go that first week, anyway? I nearly went crazy trying to find you?"

"The Garlic Festival."

"The what?"

"The Gilroy Garlic Festival. I went home . . . to Gilroy . . . and lots of good garlicky home cooking."

"You mean I wasted all that time being jealous over a garlic clove? And here I imagined you in the arms of some tall, dark, handsome stranger."

Holly couldn't stop herself from nuzzling the cheek that was so tantalizingly close to her nose. "You know I prefer blondes."

"Does that mean you'll marry this one?"

Holly was so surprised she banged his nose with her head when she looked up. "Marry? You've never mentioned getting married before."

Gingerly, he rubbed his nose. "You don't have to get violent about it. A simple 'yes' or 'whenever you're ready,' will do."

"What about 'no'? Doesn't that word fit into your scenario?"

"Not if I can help it. I'm a great believer in the power of positive thinking. Besides, you can't say no until you've listened to what was in my letters." He raised her face with the tip of his finger. "Fair?"

Holly looked into those remarkable sea-green eyes and realized she couldn't move away now even if she wanted to. And she didn't want to. With a sinking heart, she realized she never wanted to move away from him again. "Fair," she answered helplessly.

"I've given up the business, honey," he told her. "Butch Kelley's going to run it from now on. No more deep-sea diving. I'm through."

"But Kirk, I don't understand—"

"Hush, honey, hear me out. I've waited a long time to tell you this. I should have quit a long time ago. But until two months ago there was no real reason for me to quit: the money was great, I could pick my own jobs, I pretty much came and went as I pleased. It was a hard life to give up."

"Then why are you giving it up now?"

"Because for the first time in a long, long time I have something I want to live for, Holly. And every year I

184

spend in this business makes my chances of living to a ripe old age increasingly slim. The night of the storm shook me up. I've had close calls before but I could always joke about them afterwards. That night, I felt differently. I realized I didn't want to die. I wanted to live . . . with you. I wanted to have a family and some permanence. Now you and the elephant seal can make that possible."

"The elephant seal! What's he got to do with anything?"

"He showed me there's something else I can do besides get waterlogged for a living. When I stitched up that seal I felt good about myself. I hadn't touched sutures for so long, and yet it felt as if I had never let them go. I want to continue to work with ocean life, honey. Josie and I have already started to work out the details."

Holly rolled her eyes. "I'm afraid to ask how Josie got into this conversation. But tell me anyway."

"We've been playing with the idea for a while, but I told her not to mention it to you until we'd ironed out some of the problems." His eyes twinkled at her obvious confusion. "Josie and I have decided to become partners. We want to expand and modernize the aquarium and some day even computerize it so we can keep a greater variety of species. I think it can be a big success."

Holly felt dazed. "And Josie goes along with all this?"

"She thinks it's great. The other day she told me it's the first time in her life she's been propositioned by a man without any strings being attached."

Holly's heart was pounding wildly. She wanted to believe Kirk so badly it hurt. But she had to be sure.

He had to be sure. "Do you know what you're saying, Kirk? Do you realize what you'd be giving up? Diving's been your life for years."

"Only because I didn't have anything else. Now I do. Before, when I thought about medicine I pictured nose jobs and silicone breasts. Helping a defenseless animal opened up a new world for me. Honey, I can't dive forever. But I can sure spend the next thirty-odd years doing something that's just as valuable. And working with sea-life means I can still scuba dive. I'll have the best of all worlds."

"But you'll be giving up the excitement and the travel and . . . my God, Kirk, what if you get a notion to see the Pyramids or attend a *jai lai* game or . . . or . . ."

"What if I get a notion to do this . . ." His fingers played lightly over the line of her collar . . .' and you're not there? Believe me, honey, that's a much bigger loss to me than the Pyramids. Besides, by now it's a moot point. I've already sold the business to Kelley. And Josie would shoot me on sight if I reneged on her at this point."

"But the letter from the North Sea? . . . "

He grinned. "So you did look at my letters."

"Just the postmarks. Why the North Sea if you've already made all these plans?"

"If you'd looked at more than the postmark, you'd have seen I was there to wrap up my commitments. I'd signed the contracts, it was up to me to transfer them over to Kelley. I told you I'd be home in a couple of days and that I'd call." His blue-green eyes accused her. "You didn't answer the phone."

She shook her head. "No. Guess I'm a first-class coward."

"Honey, you're a first-class beauty." His kiss was

anything but tentative this time. Holly felt a warmth that could have rivaled the brightest California sunshine surge through her body. Four long weeks. It had been too long—much too long!

Kirk seemed to agree, for he suddenly released her and started the car. "Where are we going?" she asked.

"The doctor advises a brief rest at my hotel room before we proceed back to Morro Bay, Miss Bishop."

"But my car—"

"Not to worry. We'll pick it up later. First things first. Right now you need a good, strong does of rest and relaxation, Kirk Roberts's style."

"I can just bet how much R and R I'm going to get in your hotel room," she laughed.

When they stopped to wait for an opening into the line of traffic outside the garage, a bright light exploded in their faces. "Good lord, it's . . . my God, it's Mike Rafferty!" Holly rolled down her window. "Mike what in the world are you doing here?"

The Morro Bay Weekly reporter looked crestfallen. "My car broke down and I missed the session this afternoon at Worldwide Oil. I've managed to get a picture of just about everyone but you two. Have pity on a poor working guy, huh? Let me get a good picture of the two of you doing something special."

Kirk grinned. "Like this?" He put his arm around Holly and kissed her in full view of the reporter and anyone else who was lucky enough to be passing by on the busy San Francisco street.

The press camera erupted with rapid-fire brilliance, but Holly and Kirk were obliviously locked in their own little world. "Okay, you two. I've got it," Mike told them.

He stuck his head in the window. "Hey, I said you

can let up now. I've got more than I need for the next edition."

"Mmmm, but I don't," Kirk mumbled, lowering his head once again to drink the golden nectar of her sweet lips. "I'm not sure I'll ever have enough. But I'm going to spend the rest of my life working on it."

Genuine Silhouette sterling silver bookmark for only $15.95!

What a beautiful way to hold your place in your current romance! This genuine sterling silver bookmark, with the distinctive Silhouette symbol in elegant black, measures 1½″ long and 1″ wide. It makes a beautiful gift for yourself, and for every romantic you know! And, at only $15.95 each, including all postage and handling charges, you'll want to order several now, while supplies last.

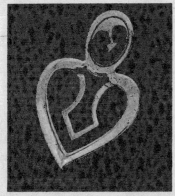

YOU'LL BE SWEPT AWAY WITH SILHOUETTE DESIRE

$1.75 each

1 ☐ James

2 ☐ Monet

3 ☐ Clay

4 ☐ Carey

5 ☐ Baker

6 ☐ Mallory

7 ☐ St. Claire

8 ☐ Dee

9 ☐ Simms

10 ☐ Smith

$1.95 each

11 ☐ James

12 ☐ Palmer

13 ☐ Wallace

14 ☐ Valley

15 ☐ Vernon

16 ☐ Major

17 ☐ Simms

18 ☐ Ross

19 ☐ James

20 ☐ Allison

21 ☐ Baker

22 ☐ Durant

23 ☐ Sunshine

24 ☐ Baxter

25 ☐ James

26 ☐ Palmer

27 ☐ Conrad

28 ☐ Lovan

29 ☐ Michelle

30 ☐ Lind

31 ☐ James

32 ☐ Clay

33 ☐ Powers

34 ☐ Milan

35 ☐ Major

36 ☐ Summers

37 ☐ James

38 ☐ Douglass

39 ☐ Monet

40 ☐ Mallory

41 ☐ St. Claire

42 ☐ Stewart

43 ☐ Simms

44 ☐ West

45 ☐ Clay

46 ☐ Chance

47 ☐ Michelle

48 ☐ Powers

49 ☐ James

50 ☐ Palmer

51 ☐ Lind

52 ☐ Morgan

53 ☐ Joyce

54 ☐ Fulford

55 ☐ James

56 ☐ Douglass

57 ☐ Michelle

58 ☐ Mallory

59 ☐ Powers

60 ☐ Dennis

61 ☐ Simms

62 ☐ Monet

63 ☐ Dee

64 ☐ Milan

65 ☐ Allison

66 ☐ Langtry

67 ☐ James

68 ☐ Browning

69 ☐ Carey

70 ☐ Victor

71 ☐ Joyce

72 ☐ Hart

73 ☐ St. Clair

74 ☐ Douglass

75 ☐ McKenna

76 ☐ Michelle

77 ☐ Lowell

78 ☐ Barber

79 ☐ Simms

80 ☐ Palmer

81 ☐ Kennedy

82 ☐ Clay

YOU'LL BE SWEPT AWAY WITH SILHOUETTE DESIRE

$1.95 each

83 ☐ Chance	97 ☐ James	111 ☐ Browning	125 ☐ Caimi
84 ☐ Powers	98 ☐ Joyce	112 ☐ Nicole	126 ☐ Carey
85 ☐ James	99 ☐ Major	113 ☐ Cresswell	127 ☐ James
86 ☐ Malek	100 ☐ Howard	114 ☐ Ross	128 ☐ Michelle
87 ☐ Michelle	101 ☐ Morgan	115 ☐ James	129 ☐ Bishop
88 ☐ Trevor	102 ☐ Palmer	116 ☐ Joyce	130 ☐ Blair
89 ☐ Ross	103 ☐ James	117 ☐ Powers	131 ☐ Larson
90 ☐ Roszel	104 ☐ Chase	118 ☐ Milan	132 ☐ McCoy
91 ☐ Browning	105 ☐ Blair	119 ☐ John	133 ☐ Monet
92 ☐ Carey	106 ☐ Michelle	120 ☐ Clay	134 ☐ McKenna
93 ☐ Berk	107 ☐ Chance	121 ☐ Browning	135 ☐ Charlton
94 ☐ Robbins	108 ☐ Gladstone	122 ☐ Trent	136 ☐ Martel
95 ☐ Summers	109 ☐ Simms	123 ☐ Paige	137 ☐ Ross
96 ☐ Milan	110 ☐ Palmer	124 ☐ St. George	138 ☐ Chase

SILHOUETTE DESIRE, Department SD/6
1230 Avenue of the Americas
New York, NY 10020

Please send me the books I have checked above. I am enclosing $_____
(please add 75¢ to cover postage and handling. NYS and NYC residents please
add appropriate sales tax). Send check or money order—no cash or C.O.D.'s
please. Allow six weeks for delivery.

NAME_____

ADDRESS_____

CITY_____STATE/ZIP_____